Mairi's Wedding
By Andrew Hendry

A Novel by Peter Stickland

Foreword by Marie-Anne Mancio

77 books

This novel is a tribute to Neil Munro

The author has used numerous quotations from the novels and stories of Neil Munro in this modern day romance and much of the language is inspired by Munro's delightful lyricism.

Published in Great Britain, 2009 by 77 books
69 Osbaldeston Road, London N16 7DL

www.77books.co.uk

Copyright © Peter Stickland 2009
The author has asserted his right under the Copyright, Designs and Patents Act, 1988 to be identified as the author of this work.

ISBN 978-0-9560121-3-5

This book is sold subject to the condition that it shall not by way of trade or otherwise, be lent, resold, hired out, or otherwise circulated without the publisher's prior consent in any form of binding or cover other than that in which it is published and without a similar condition including this condition being imposed on the subsequent purchaser.

The front cover painting is by Louise Blair.
Book design and layout by Dennis Mariner.

For Mairi, Don, Ria, Louise and Cordelia

'From the outset it was apparent that someone had played a colossal trick on something. The switches had been tripped, as it were; the entire world or one's limited but accurate idea of it was bathed in glowing love, of a sort that need never have come into being but was now indispensable as air is to living creatures.'

John Ashbery, from *Three Poems*

A Note from Ronnie Renton, chairman of the Neil Munro Society.

Lesley Lendrum, the granddaughter and biographer of Neil Munro, and The Neil Munro Society are delighted that the writings of Neil Munro have been the inspiration for *Mairi's Wedding By Andrew Hendry*. The use of such a substantial amount of quotation from Neil Munro is in itself a tribute to him and a clear indication of the author's admiration of his work.

Mairi's Wedding, written in a modern and experimental manner, is unusual in the Scottish literary tradition, but it is greatly welcomed and we hope it will bring Neil Munro to a totally different and wider readership.

Acknowledgements

To have had the support of Marie-Anne Mancio during the writing of this novel was a luxury. A perfect indication of the warmth and intelligence of her contribution can be gleaned from the insights she offers in her foreword. I am deeply indebted to Clare Carolan for her enthusiastic response to the novel and for her editorial advice. Her contribution to many aspects of its fine tuning both in terms of detail and content kept the spirit of it alive to the end. I am also indebted to Ronnie Renton for discussing this book with the family of Neil Munro and members of the Neil Munro Society and for his numerous suggestions that were taken up during the final editing process.

My thanks are also due to Dennis Mariner, whose commitment to the design and layout was, as always, generous; to Julian Maynard Smith, whose company is always a pleasure; to Joy Flanagan who expressed her delight in these pages so poignantly; to Andrea Parry for proof-reading; to Georgia Mancio who inspired my words about Annie the jazz singer; to Guillermo Rozenthuler who has inspired my listening and to Martin Green, who by chance, one fine evening, leaped to his library shelves and handed me a novel by Neil Munro.

Contents

Part 1
The Gathering

1	Finlay	
5	Cordelia	
9	Esther	
13	Clyde	
17	Mairi	
21	Andrew	
25	Alastair	
29	Christine	
33	Ethan	
37	Donald	
41	Aileen	
45	Murdo	
49	James	
53	Duncan	
57	Cathy	
61	Craig	
65	Mary	
69	Neil	
73	Annie	
77	Eilidh	
81	Sebastian	
85	Flora	
89	Emile	
93	Alban	

Part 2
The Wedding

100	Intrigue And Sabotage
103	A Sudden Connection
106	The First Day Of Spring
109	As The Moon Throws The Clouds Apart
112	A Voyage Of Ecstasy
115	Awakened By Music
118	Too Much To Lose
121	A Salve For A Sore Heart
124	In A Flame Of Colour
127	The Soaring Lark
130	Running On Fairy Isles
133	Where Comes No Grief Or Ageing
136	References to the Novels of Neil Munro

Foreword

Marie-Anne Mancio

In this foreword I refer to the novel's title as *Mairi's Wedding*, its title in the narrative, rather than the full published title, *Mairi's Wedding By Andrew Hendry*. The reason for this will become clear.

A foreword to *Mairi's Wedding* already exists elsewhere in this book but you'll have to wait until you reach page sixty-five to read it. In a strategy typical of Peter Stickland's playful attention to meta-fiction, Mary, one of the characters, is writing it for a book that is to be a wedding gift to Mairi. In the narrative, the novel is the creation of three authors; Andrew the intended, Mairi's brother-in-law Finlay, and Ethan, a guest who has travelled to the Scottish Highlands for the event. It is they who decide the author should be called 'Andrew Hendry' (a marriage of bride and groom's names) 'so that no known person can be credited with writing it'.

The other 'unofficial' foreword to *Mairi's Wedding* might be the entire output of one of Scotland's most loved authors, Neil Munro, whose words and spirit infuse both the real and the fictional novels presented here. Munro is mentioned early on as Mairi lends *Gilian The Dreamer* to her friend, Esther as the best introduction she has to the Scottish landscape. Enchanted, Esther then passes the novel to her twin brother Ethan. Both landscapes – the fictive and the real – soon become conflated. There's even a character called Clyde (a reference perhaps to the subject of Munro's travelogue *The Clyde, River And Firth*) whose erroneous map-reading takes him to Dunderawe Castle, Loch Fyne, the setting of Munro's third novel *Doom Castle*.

Munro was born in nearby Inverary in 1863 and though his paternity was never officially declared, local lore says he was related to the Duke of Argyll. His mother Ann was a kitchen maid at the Duke's castle in Inverary and she took him to live with his maternal grandmother on a farm in Glen Aray. He had local schooling until the age of thirteen so never attended university; his knowledge of Gaelic derived from his family and he was self-taught in Latin after a stint as a clerk in a lawyer's office. Just before he turned eighteen he moved to Glasgow to find employment and worked as a journalist for various papers including *The Glasgow News*, *The Falkirk Herald* and as chief reporter at *The Glasgow Evening News*. He wrote his popular, humorous stories about Para Handy, Master Mariner of the puffer Vital Spark under the pseudonym of Hugh Foulis in order to separate them from what he thought of as his 'serious' fiction. The latter included nine, primarily historical, novels one of which was unfinished, beginning in 1898 with *John Splendid* serialised in *Blackwood's Magazine*. Set in 1645, the story examines the effect of social turmoil on the Highland psyche. His last, highly accomplished novel *The New Road* (1914) displays his ambivalence towards the increasing changes in Highland life. Whilst ostensibly about a man's search to unravel the circumstances of his father's death, it recognises the contemporary necessity for progress whilst simultaneously lamenting the erosion of centuries old traditions.

Despite his success, critical appreciation for Munro was not unanimous. Poet-philosopher Hugh MacDiarmid, arguably the instigator of the Scottish Renaissance, lamented Munro's parochialism claiming, '[he] literally has no place in British, let alone European literature: he simply does not count – his popularity – is simply a commercial phenomenon, an element [...] in contemporary entertainment.'[1] By the time of his death in 1930, Munro had received an honorary doctorate from the University of Glasgow and was being hailed as the heir to the Scottish literary throne, after Walter Scott and Robert Louis Stevenson. Yet by the 1980s his novels were all out of print, only the Para Handy stories televised by the BBC still available in paperback. It is thanks to the dedication of the Neil Munro Society (who also feature in *Mairi's Wedding*) and to the role played by academia in promoting Scottish Literature that Munro is now credited for his innovative subversion of the kailyard fiction[2] of J. M. Barrie, Ian MacClaren, and S. R. Crockett which predominated.

---

1 'Neil Munro' in Hugh MacDiarmid *Contemporary Scottish Studies*, ed. Alan Riach, (Manchester: Carcanet, 1992) pp. 18-19.
2 Kitchen-garden, from the Gaelic word 'kail', meaning cabbage. Short-lived but vastly popular in Britain and America, late

Munro's interrogation of the Romantic myth of the Highlander is echoed in this novel, both celebrated (through such characters as Black Duncan and Craig, the piper from Uist) and mocked (Clyde 'imagines bands of uncouth, tartan clad natives lurking behind the trees and he hears their whispers delivered in a jargon that is entirely unknown to him'). Yet there is the air of a fairytale about *Mairi's Wedding*. It is a world populated with artists: Cathy is a painter; Mairi produces records; the characters choose the title *Mairi's Wedding* because of 'the ring of familiarity it gains from being associated with the popular song'; Cordelia sings; Ethan, Finlay, and Andrew write; Clyde invents stories... – artists who have or provoke discussions about structure and mathematics, about the function of narrative, about the role of chance and accidents, about illusion and myth. Mundane decisions do not occupy or concern them but then there are no grand dramas, no contorted plot devices either. Even Mairi's threat to 'call the whole thing off unless [she] can arrange for something magical to occur' does not worry us unduly because magic always seems possible.

The conversations among the writers in *Mairi's Wedding* about their proposed book may well anticipate objections

---

nineteenth-century trend in sentimental fiction (the city is a place of danger) in which communities in mostly remote rural settings worked together to combat troubles. Noted for its bourgeois ideology – the respectable family prevails – that ignores real social problems and for the use of Scots dialect.

to the author's liberal use of Munro's language. He might cite just the odd phrase or at other points whole paragraphs are taken and re-sited (or recited) in new contexts. As Mary describes, '*Sometimes the text elaborates upon or extends a theme and at other times its presence is used to create dissonance or surprise. Some quotes are given name or gender changes to ensure they fit and other quotes are left intact.*' To many, this is an audacious act of plagiarism. Even if current critical thinking prefers the word *appropriation* and even with such conceptually sophisticated, twentieth-century defences as Wimsatt and Beardsley's 1946 theory of intentional fallacy which claims a text is 'detached from the author at birth and goes about the world beyond his power to intend about it or control it,' or Roland Barthes' seminal essay *The Death Of The Author*, (1967) – plagiarism remains a dirty word.

But what constitutes a plagiarist? Are they a paraphraser like Bruno Bettelheim, (*The Uses Of Enchantment*) whom *Newsweek* eventually dubbed Bruno *Borrow*heim? Are they a translator, copy-and-paster, ghost writer? Or a cryptomnesiac? An avid reader writing under the influence of their favourite author? Both T. S. Eliot and Ezra Pound called their liftings *collage*, and in her foreword, Mary describes *Mairi's Wedding* the same way. Even Julius E. Heuscher (from whom Bettelheim allegedly borrowed) was gracious enough to say, 'Some ideas become so true to you that they become your own.'[3] It is not inconceivable

---

[3] *Newsweek*, February 18, 1991

that Munro's attitude would have been similar. Plagiarism did not have a moral dimension in the nineteenth century. As long as sources were acknowledged and thoughtfully used, and the resulting text was not satirical, it was perfectly acceptable to incorporate others' writing. If anything, the practice was one of stealth since the new version was supposed to contain seamlessly integrated text. Acknowledgment could be implicit, relying on the educated reader's recognition of the original; as Tilar J. Mazzeo notes: 'Ironically, the more extensive the borrowing the more likely it was to have been considered acknowledged.'[4]

Unconscious plagiarism was also forgivable in the nineteenth century, an attitude shared by Ethan who argues, '*as far as I am aware I write without knowledge or forethought. If I am driving over a Scottish moor and mud and grass become attached to my car should I be accused of stealing it? I didn't choose what stuck to my car and if I decide to sell it without cleaning it, or without editing the content, have I to credit the Highlands Authority first?*' The line between borrowing and theft is ambiguous though, at worst leaving in its wake possibly great, unwritten works by authors who saw the critical or financial rewards for their efforts go to someone else (did the Harvard-Oxford-Sorbonne-educated T. S. Eliot deliberately steal *The Wasteland* from Madison Cawein, a pool hall cashier who saved up for six years to fund

---

4 *Plagiarism And Literary Property In The Romantic Period*, (Pennsylvannia: University of Pennsylvannia Press, 2007) p.3.

his poetry? Were the thesis, phrases, and mistakes in H. G. Wells' *The Outline Of History* reproduced from an earlier, unpublished manuscript by Florence Deeks as she alleged?). But at its best, borrowing is a cultural exchange. The act of loaning something that belongs to us often makes us look at it in a new way. An item of clothing assumes a different shape when someone else tries it on; the same musical phrase can sound even more alluring when sung by another. By the same token, what, or whom, we choose to borrow is always revealing. When we give something back, it is not necessarily in the same condition as before.

Mairi's Wedding borrows from Neil Munro in order to invite us to return to him, so, for the uninitiated, the novel acts as an induction to his literature (when Ethan buys all the Munro titles he can in a second-hand bookstore, the short story collections – *The Lost Pibroch, Jaunty Jock,* and *Ayrshire Idylls* – are there too). For long-time lovers of Munro, *Mairi's Wedding* could be as pleasurable a read as the originals. We begin to wonder which of his works have been plundered or perhaps to recognise old favourites; we try to excavate sources: is this from *The Daft Days* or *John Splendid*? From *The New Road* or *Gilian The Dreamer*? Reading *Mairi's Wedding* is almost a reading in parallel, like falling in love (again) with two texts at the same time.

A few months before beginning *Heart Of Darkness* in 1898, Joseph Conrad was a guest of Dr. John McIntyre – the first person to x-ray the human heart; he recalled discussing the secret of the universe 'while Neil Munro stood in front of a Rontgen machine and on the screen behind we contemplated his backbone and his ribs'.[5] Stickland examines Munro like this and seems to get to the very bones of him. His judicious placing of borrowed gems such as: *'so daft about her, she could lead him round the country with a cobweb, – that's the way with men before ye marry them'* or *'willow-wrens laced the bushes with a filigree of song so fine it would have missed the ear of a traveller less observant. Life! Life! – Lord, how he felt the sting and splendour of it in his every sense!'* – amid the clarity of his own prose – alert us to the fact that though Munro's poetry was less distinctive he was an intensely poetic writer.

But literary qualities aside, what, other than their love of the Highland spirit, does Stickland see in him? Why interpose a late nineteenth/early twentieth century author celebrated for his historical fiction into a twenty-first century novel? One answer is that Munro is slippery, not easy to categorise. His career straddled two eras: one marked by a *fin de siècle* sensibility, the other by early modernism. He wrote historically in order to comment on his present, and anticipated the interwar shift in Scotland's literature. He may not have approved of the Anglicisation of the Highlands that began in the eighteenth century, but he was sufficiently pragmatic to modify his use of dialect thus instantly making his writing more accessible. His fiction is characterised by the liminal, something Stickland makes explicit in this novel by never altering

---

5   Letter to Edward Garnett, 29th September 1898.

the grammatical tense of quotations. Mary – my writer in parallel – observes, this can work '*against the language construction of the piece in which it is placed, a device that will either strain readers or invite them to enjoy collision, a choice that is the readers*'. This brings us to the other underlying constant of the book: its structure. Stickland hints at his game through Andrew (Mairi's future husband). Like Munro, Andrew has a background in journalism but now finds himself without opinions. When he writes, he '*edits his words so that they fill the whole page and the intensity of his geometry as he nears the end remains as charged as ever. If his last line does not take up the entire width of the page then he looks for an alternative word, sentence or layout strategy to ensure that it does*'. As Esther would say, '*Have you ever heard anything so beautiful?*'

Marie-Anne Mancio

Dramatis Personae

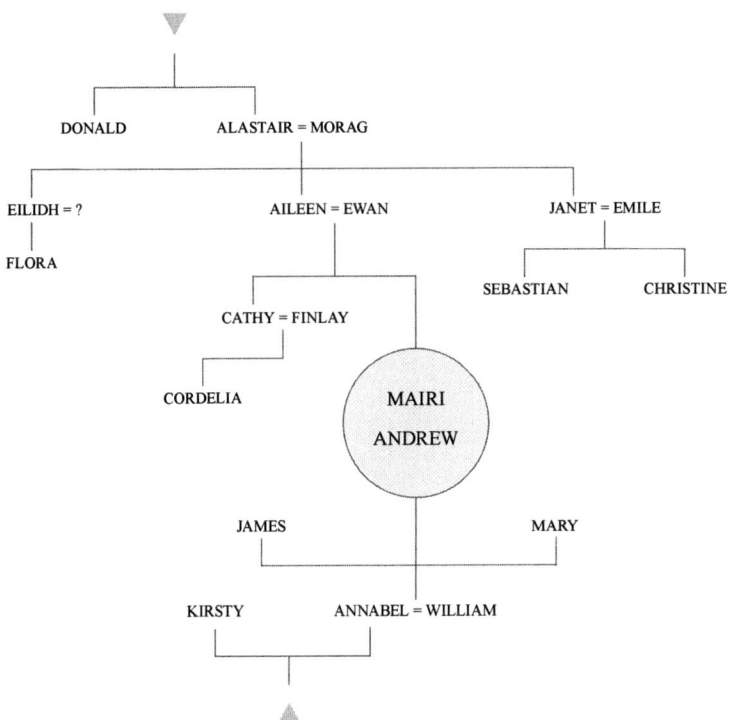

MAIRI'S FAMILY

ANDREW'S FAMILY

FRIENDS OF BRIDE AND GROOM

Esther and Ethan (twins), Neil, Clyde, Annie.

OTHER CHARACTERS

Duncan, Captain of the boat;
Murdo, Donald's friend;
Craig, Piper; Coll, Piper's son;
Alban, School teacher's son.

Part 1

The Gathering

Finlay

Mairi and Cathy, being sisters, have qualities that are similar and of these it is the meddling with other people's lives that is most significant. They practise their art with the best intentions and in very different ways, but whenever their gaze is directed at the same cause, which is common enough, they rarely agree about who should take responsibility. It is Mairi's claim that Cathy starts everything and then gives her the credit to avoid the attention it receives; it is Cathy's claim that Mairi, being more energetically engaged, is the one to promote ideas abroad and give some assurance to the possibilities of their success.

Cathy, a painter who spends much of her time in the studio, accepts the kind of mess that paint makes to avoid any notion of this kind of mess in her life; having control of her world is her trusted pathway to a peaceful existence. By contrast Mairi's studio is dedicated to sound and when she is not producing records consequences are not a thing she stops to consider; she can take up an idea and proceed with its resolution before Cathy has even found the correct words to express it. It is common for both to expect others to comply with their demands and generally this is what happens.

Mairi has ambitions for her wedding day and many arrangements have been made to satisfy these, but as the day draws near Cathy, feeling a little under employed, has decided that the occasion would benefit from a few extra surprises. One of these, a present for the married couple, is a photo album containing photographs and written portraits of the guests. She has no intention of producing the work herself, preferring instead to have her husband, Finlay write the words and her future brother-in-law's brother, James to take the photographs. For Finlay the written task is an enterprise full of unforeseen pitfalls, but he has not expressed his concern rigorously enough for Cathy to take note of it. James on the other hand was eager to please and appeared to accept his photographic brief with some enthusiasm.

When Cathy appeared in Finlay's study one afternoon she was alerted to her husband's sudden response. He clicked out of one file and opened another with the portraits on it before she could see the computer screen.

'Have you come to see how the biographies are progressing?' he asked and Cathy said she had. Finlay was relieved that his speedy shift of activity wasn't detected or at the least that his secrecy was regarded as acceptable. Even the accusation that he practices clandestine habits is more acceptable to him than an admission to his wife that he is at the writing once more. Cathy read the portraits, expressed her satisfaction in them and complained again about the precious few guests who had responded to her call for information. She then asked Finlay about the writing he was engaged in.

'Och, I'm just fiddling,' he replied, 'there's nought of any consequence in it.'

'That's not a reason to avoid telling me,' Cathy said. 'I am certain it's a story you're on.'

'Well it's a story right enough, but I've no clue what happens in it.'

'Well, if you ask me, I suspect, that not having a clue is important to you.'

'True, true,' Finlay admited, 'it's how I surprise myself. You can be certain that if I don't surprise myself then I'll not surprise you or any other folk who might read it.'

Cathy pondered this remark and while she was intent upon not saying anything that might discourage him she couldn't help but address the issue of structure.

'You must have some idea that you're working towards. How will you know if you're being honest or saying something relevant?' Finlay shrugged. 'You will not know if a thing is missing if there is no structure to support it. It's those little things that come to mind when clarifying issues that makes the meaningful connections.'

'Well, if it comes to that, I have something in mind, but it has little to do with structure, it's more like a feeling I have, but it helps with the decisions right enough.'

Cathy prompted him to say more, but Finlay, thinking hard, could only sigh in response. There was nothing he wanted to say, but Cathy waited for his answer.

'It's just that I am trying not to be judgemental about the characters. I want to reveal them in a kindly light and have them proud of their achievements, just as we all are when it's recognised that we have done a thing well. I want them to feel pleased and grateful that nothing more is required, that they can take time off as a reward, without worrying whether others will start to feel crabby about their luck.'

Cathy wore a puzzled look.

'Indeed,' Finlay continued, 'I want everyone to work together to express their appreciation of all that their fellow characters have achieved.'

'It's a strange ambition,' Cathy responded, 'to write of characters without faults.'

'Och, faults they have right enough, but they're accepted. D'ye not think that the more acceptances we practice the happier we are? Sometimes all a body has to say is 'thank you' rather than 'explain yourself,' to promote the good feelings, and if such pleasantries could connect to the centre of things and the gentle things ripple out from there to touch everyone, then I want to be around to describe their surprise and record their laughter.'

'Are you certain about the laughter?' Cathy asked.

'Well, it's the kind of laughter that accompanies startlement, the kind of thing folk feel when something is just, when it's exactly how they imagined it could be, rather than the way they feared it. You know how it is when a thing we do well isn't at all difficult to achieve and it makes us laugh, just for the joy of it?'

There are times when Cathy finds her husband the most bewildering of souls. It was not an easy matter for her to find the right questions to put to him. As she made her way to the kitchen to prepare supper, she sent her daughter a text to remind her that it was time she was heading home.

Cordelia

It has always happened that the first steps of a boy from the glen have been to the quay. There the ships lie clumsily on their bulging sides in the ebb till the tar steams and blisters in the sun, or at the full they lift and fall heavily like a sigh for the ocean's expanse as they feel themselves prisoners to the rings and pawls. Their chains jerk and ease upon the granite edges of the wall or twang tight across the quay so that the mariners and fishermen, moving about their business on this stone thrust to the sea, must lift their clumping boots high to step across those tethers of romance.[1]

Young Cordelia is no tomboy, but after a visit to the quay with her great grandfather she felt the lure of the place. For her the quay positively reeked of romance and as far as romance is concerned Cordelia is a proposition to be reckoned with. Alastair, Cordelia's great grandfather, owned a boat that traded between the islands and after he had introduced his great granddaughter to the skipper of this boat, a man by the name of Black Duncan, Cordelia would be at the quay whenever Duncan's boat was in. Together they could while away the hours free of the restraint they felt in other folk's company.

The secret of Cordelia's attraction to Duncan is that he made her light-minded and serious at the same time, causing her thoughts to run deep. In his company she felt alert and beautiful – or gleg and braw as we might say hereabouts – and there's not a sweeter lass anywhere that's more deserving of the sailor's inspiration. Cordelia blossomed in the old mariner's company and she in turn inspired him. He was not the adventurer he made out to be, but a Skye-man who can stay long in his fancy and make the simplest of ventures a riot of fearful and risky delights for Cordelia's young ears.

When Black Duncan learned that Cordelia possessed a beautiful singing voice it was the start of many things. The first was that he began teaching her his repertoire of songs and then, once he had the full measure of her lyrical resonance, he began teaching her the old Gaelic. The young girl had a surprising talent for it.

'How is it that words and a tune should endure, unchangin', when all else alters?' he would ask and each time he asked it Cordelia would attempt an answer. She never succeeded at solving his riddle, but they spent many an hour pondering it. One day Duncan taught Cordelia to sing *Auburn Lass*, or *Nighean rua' bhàn* as it is in the Gaelic, and when she was finished there were tears in the old mariner's eyes.

Auburn Donald's Piper's auburn lass,
She would go to a ball if she got a fiddler.
Auburn Donald's Piper's auburn lass,
She would make peace if she got a dram.
She would tease, she would comb.

She would go to a ball if she got a fiddler.
She would tease, she would comb.
She would make peace if she got a dram.

Cordelia's singing was a glamour and a charm to Duncan and he knew for certain that it would affect other hearts in a similar manner. One day, with the full poetic mood upon him, Duncan stirred his memory, alerted his imagination and came up with a tale that he claimed to have heard from his one time first mate, Jimmy Dyce. Cordelia listened to the old mariner without moving a muscle. This was his story.

'On a day, when Jimmy were a lad and lost upon the sea, he came upon the port of Erin, a place that'll ne'er be visited by inteention. To find Erin ye must sail wi' the winds and drift i' the calms and when all hope o' findin' it is lost you might deesco'er it. For some folk Erin is a place to gi'e ye the croodles and creeps the very moment ye een is upon't, but for others it's a place as sweet as returnin' hame.

'Jimmy's hackles rose when his wayward boat drifted t'wards an openin' i' the rocks, for the scene before 'im wasna any different to Erin's Eye, as he'd heard tell of it. He shivered as his boat was sucked in through an openin' i' the rocks and into a bay. Then, as he was sailin' roond a dark mountain, as the sort that rises up out o' the sea, his nerves were fit to bust, for he came to a cove with the magical port of Erin lying there before 'im.

'Jimmy tied his boat to the quay and stood upon the dock listenin' to the soond o' Gaelic chords that were all aboot him. He asked o' a passing sailor from whare the soonds were comin' and the mariner's reply was that they were comin' from all roond.

'Recognisin' the worrisome look on Jimmy's face he told 'im, "Och its nay sae bad laddie, Erin's like many a port. It's the unfortunate anes who doont hare the chords, d'ya ken?" Jimmy nodded. "Well, being as you do then you'd best keep an ear oot for the sangin' o' the king's daughter, for ye'll ne'er hare such wondrous sounds to accompany the minor keys as her voice can mak' it."

'The mariner went on 'is way, leavin' Jimmy a little beweeldered. At first the young fellow couldna ken what was to be doin' with he'sel', but after a night i' the tavern and we a fine breakfast inside him, Jimmy took he'sel' on a walk through the toon with Gaelic chords fir company.

'The townsfolk were gay and wished 'im well, but they were each mighty surpreesed when Jimmy caught a glimpse o' the king's daughter after only a few minutes. She was standin' on the castle terrace combin' her hair and Jimmy stood watchin' like a transfeexed man. Then the king's daughter started on her singing and the voice o' her cast a glamour o'er the een o' our spectator.

'Once she had finished, all they aboot the young man cried out to 'im, "Call a woman's name Jimmy, any name," and Jimmy called out the name Susan. He had known a Susan at school and he had liked her well enough, but he couldna think why he might be sayin' her name just then. "Then it's Susan ye shall marry", the toonsfolk told him, "and as she's not livin' heeraboot then you'd best be back on your boat to look for her", and before the sun was high oor Jimmy was sailin' oot to sea, headin' fer hame.'

Esther

Having settled herself in a seat facing in the direction the train was moving Esther opened the book Mairi had given her for the journey. 'It is the best introduction I can give you,' Mairi had told her.

Ethan was sitting opposite his sister with his eyes closed, nursing some arrant irresolution that was sticking insistently to his creative ambitions. There were times when he considered it a foolish thing to harbour such a singular obsession with writing, but this glaiked spirit of his was the thing that helped him diminish his moods, that enabled him to transpose his despondency into something more akin to inspiration. When irresolution wasn't beckoning, Ethan could fly.

'Listen to this,' Esther nudged him. 'Mairi's book reads like a dream.'

Ethan opened his eyes and sighed.

'*It was the spring: the larch was hung with tassels; all the woods were sweet with the tang of pine, the chuckling thrush, and the flurry of honeymoon wings. There had been rain in the early morning; no speck of dust was on the world, as clean as if it had been new created, and the burns ran merrily, merrily, twitching in fun at the lower flounces of the lady ferns that bent over them. Each mossy cliff dropped gems, and every dyke was burning with the pale flame of primroses that grow in Schawfield as they grow no otherwhere, – so soon, so long, so unmolested, as if a primrose crop were the single aim of nature.'* [2]

'Have you ever heard anything so beautiful?' Esther asked and Ethan shook his head.

'Who is the author?'

'Neil Munro. Do you think that Mairi's landscape will be anything like the one he describes?'

'The season now is summer, not spring,' Ethan reminded her. Esther returned to her book. 'Did Neil Munro begin his book with the passage you read?' Esther shook her head and continued reading to him.

'Along the hunting roads where the hoofs of the horse sank soundless in the turf, the coney scuttled and the foumart flashed. A ruddy patch of hide was stirring in the thicket; he saw the dappled fallow nibble leaves in the enchanted clearings; wood doves murmured; willow-wrens laced the bushes with a filigree of song so fine it would have missed the ear of a traveller less observant. Life! Life! – Lord, how he felt the sting and splendour of it in his every sense!' [2]

'I could almost weep,' Esther exclaimed. 'Could you write like this?'

'Huh,' was Ethan's expletive. He sighed again and turned his gaze to the uninspiring scenery. Esther continued reading to herself quietly.

'It's just not possible, not these days at any rate.'

'What isn't?' Esther asked.

'Writing like this, you know, with fine descriptive

phrases and the poetic spirit so prominently displayed. Everything is against it.'

'It depends,' she insisted. 'I'm sure you could do it if you found the idea intriguing enough.'

'I couldn't. I couldn't have written like that at the time, when the culture was alive to such possibilities, and I certainly couldn't do it now.' Esther didn't answer him. 'Anyway, the beginnings are always the easy part; it's the rest that's difficult. You may be expecting too much of your Mr. Munro. Come the next chapter he might be offering you his self-righteous sentiments and his predictable dialogue.'

'No he won't. He cares nothing for judgements, only for his simple means and he offers these to us lightly; fine sentiments and the making of connections, these are the things for him. Oh! How I love it.' Esther started to read aloud again and Ethan listened attentively.

'For a moment he checked the mare, took off his wide grey hat, and, breathing deep of the landward breeze, stared at the archipelago. Silver and green, with the pillars of birches and their tender plumage, the lesser isles were lying like fairy gardens in the Sound, and far away – far, far away, – sailing among the sunset's gold, were the great isles of the Hebrides. He looked upon them like their first discoverer – a lean man, a clean man, smirched by no town reek nor sallowed by greasy foods, late hours, and the breathed atmosphere of herded populations; tan and ruddy, satin-skinned, brown-haired; an eye that quested like an eagle's, and swooped on distant things as does the seaman's eye or the old hunter's.'[2]

'I wish he were describing you,' Esther said, smiling.

'Do you?' Ethan asked. 'You would like me to be a man of the landscape then?'

'Yes. No,' Esther checked herself, quickly. 'I wouldn't like you to pretend that you were, but I should like you to be closer to the origins of your emotions.'

'Mmm,' Ethan mumbled. 'I've probably breathed in too much of the atmosphere of herded populations for that and being too much sallowed by greasy foods and late nights I would have to abstain before qualifying.'

'Oh, don't take it to heart. You're fine at your ideas, but sometimes ideas have too much purpose in them and purpose always has dominion over imagination.'

'I hope he doesn't disappoint you,' Ethan remarked.

'You've a slight grudge to your tone, Ethan.'

'But he might, it happens often enough.'

'Well, I'll let you know if he does. These are simple stories and the man loves plain pleasures, I doubt that he will sacrifice these qualities for another purpose.'

Esther returned to her reading, but as the sighs coming from Ethan were ever more present she asked if he had brought anything with him to read.

'Yes, but I don't feel like reading right now.'

'Would you like to read this?' she asked, holding out her book to him.

'Yes, I would, just to get a flavour of it you understand.' Esther handed him the book. 'Thank you. Are you sure? I don't want to spoil your pleasure.'

'Sure,' she said, 'go ahead, I'll read it soon enough.' She smiled at him knowingly before closing her eyes.

Clyde

Having been invited to the Highlands to celebrate his friend's wedding, Clyde decided to travel up by car so that he could enjoy something of the landscape before Andrew's important day. On the day of his departure, Clyde started out early, determined to be far from any city by nightfall, but in the late afternoon he made a poor map reading decision. On paper it looked like a short cut, but the reality was far from this; the road itself might better be described as a rough track, and this track was taking him up a steep incline into a great expanse of open moorland.

When Clyde was at the summit he was struck by the beauty of the sun lying low in the sky and he revised his view of the decision he took earlier, but a little later still, when his car had stopped in the middle of nowhere and refused to start again, Clyde reverted to his previous opinion. His mobile phone had no reception and there were neither cars, dwellings or people to be seen.

Clyde, undeterred, continued his journey on foot and reverted to his favourite pastime; the invention of stories. The moorland gradually became a landscape thick with trees as he moved solemnly down the slope. Here he imagined gaunt forms in the undergrowth and the sounds of the wood's inhabitants caused trepidation in him. He imagined bands of uncouth, tartan clad natives lurking behind the trees and he heard their whispers delivered in a jargon that was entirely unknown to him.

Clyde had lived with stories in his head since he could first remember and their presence was as natural to him as the air he breathed. 'He is forever in a dream,' his mother had said when anyone asked after him and, if she needed his attention when the dreams were upon him, she would coax him gently from his imaginative world as though he were a child lost in sleep walking. Clyde had told his mother about his dialogue with phantoms, with animals, and objects and she understood that he could read anything into the cracks on walls or the patterns on curtains. She also assumed that it was quite usual for a healthy, creative boy, who spent most his days reading, to engage such dreams and imaginings.

After travelling down the glen for a while, Clyde began to lose hope, began to doubt that he would ever find habitation, so he started running, both to get somewhere sooner and to get away from the imagined inhabitants who pursued him from the woods. The noises only got more intrusive as he proceeded and soon our hero became exhausted from the running. He stopped, turned about and addressed the forest. 'Come out and talk,' he invited them, affecting a cheerfulness he did not feel, 'my bag has nothing of worth in it and my clothes will not keep you warm.' He would have bantered on, but on hearing another sound close by, he turned again, sharply this time and, stumbling in a rut, he fell to the ground.

It was when Clyde was first at school that his mother became aware of his propensity for accidents. He was a tall boy, but at play his movements were entirely flexible, gymnastic even, so it was a mystery to her that Clyde could finish the day with endless cuts from falling over and bumping into things. 'Just look at him,' his mother would entreat her friends, 'why should one of nature's best specimens, a boy who moves like a gazelle, have nothing but accidents.' Clyde responded with his generous open smile and gave no evidence to account for his bruises.

The truth of it for Clyde, and this is something that he kept to himself, was that these accidents were not of his own making, but rather the clumsy acts of a god who allowed the world's flora and fauna to conspire against him. There were possible grounds for this belief, for lightning had already struck him twice and he was frequently stung by wasps or nettles that others could not see. On one occasion he was bitten by a spider and was rushed to hospital with a dangerously swollen leg.

Clyde, relieved that he had no more than a few scrapes from his tumble, continued his walk in a somewhat lonely and disconsolate way. Then, while longing for the landscape to become silent, he heard the sound of waves breaking against rocks and his spirits lifted. A breeze was getting up and as he turned a bend he saw a road resembling a busy highway. With his imagined pistol he fired a parting shot into the woods to warn off his pursuers and strutted along the road, free, singing and laughing.

Such jollity is another of Clyde's characteristics. Surprisingly, it wasn't one that won him friends at school, but he always stuck with it. Despite his unbelievable kind-heartedness, the other boys preferred teasing him and making him the subject of their jokes, rather than having him as an ally. It was, of course, important to Clyde that he won their approval and when he realised that he could achieve this by playing the fool, he developed his acrobatic, accident-prone performance with such mastery that he eventually earned their esteem and the affectionate nickname 'Jester'.

After strutting along for a while, Clyde spied a castle standing proudly ahead of him and he broke into a run. When he saw a light shining from a tower he whooped for joy, but once he was around the next bend, upon the edge of the sea, he realised that the castle stood some way from the shoreline by some twenty metres or more. He watched the waves lapping around it, but rather than stand bewildered, he scrambled over the rocks, took off his shoes, rolled up his trousers and waded through the mud towards the islet. Once upon it, the sight of the ominous fortress prompted his narrative voice to rise up again and this time he imagined himself an ancient adventurer. Making his way over a patch of garden-ground at the front of the castle he came to a large door and here he stopped to consider his next move. He studied the door for some time to rehearse how he might make his entrance. Over the arch, ponderous and deep-moulded, hung a scowling eyebrow of black and studded oak, and above this was an escutcheon with a blazon of hands around an embattled castle. The legend read, *'Doom. Man Behauld the End of All. Be Nocht Wiser than the Hiest. Hope in God!'* [3]

Mairi

Before going to the kitchen to prepare supper, Cathy sent her daughter a text that read, 'Supper in thirty minutes.' It was certain that Cordelia would not return on time unless she was prompted to do so. Cathy set about the task of peeling vegetables and while reflecting upon the wandering nature of her husband's inspiration it occured to her that Finlay's way of proceeding was not dissimilar to Mairi's, particularly in the lack of planning that was evident in her wedding preparations. Curiously enough Finlay, while closing down his computer, was having exactly the same thought at the very same time.

Cathy's pots were boiling happily when Cordelia entered the kitchen with her Aunt Mairi. Cathy kissed her sister and invited her to stay for supper, which Mairi graciously accepted. Once she had a glass of wine in her hand, Mairi gave expression to the frustrations she was experiencing over the wedding celebrations.

'I'm going to call the whole thing off unless I can arrange for something magical to occur,' she told them. Cordelia smiled and Cathy frowned.

'What are you wanting now that's not happening?' Cathy asked.

'Everything that's important,' Mairi moaned. 'I have

achieved nothing but the dull fact of having invited a good many friends and family to the same place at the same time. Eating and drinking is fine as far as it goes, but something else must occur. I must be able to put on something that will entertain my guests. I want to excite their nervous systems a little.'

Finlay entered and hearing Mairi's remark, he enquired if she had managed to arrange the music yet.

'I have searched everywhere,' Mairi complained. 'It's wretched that Annie can't play for us. I am now left with a *céilidh* band who will make the thing a jigging party. Aunt Eilidh knows plenty of folk who sing and she is keen to help, but something tells me this is not the way to do it, that I should be finding the music by luck. It's as if this were the only way that my guests would be able to feel that they are hearing these sounds for the first time. I want the music to have enough resonance in it to halt those things in us that go along automatically.'

Cathy did not perceive the possibility her sister referred to and she regarded it an ambition not born of the highlands. Finlay nodded and Cordelia smiled.

'What happens after your guests have had their continuum halted,' Cathy asked.

'I don't know, but now and then its good for us to empty ourselves of that great unconscious enterprise of keeping going just for the sake of keeping going. There are times when the ancient Gaelic sounds can put new heart in a body.'

Cathy pulled pans out of the cupboard noisily and told her sister that she was far too much of the mists and mountains for her own good. Finlay, albeit silently, confirmed his affinity with his sister-in-law's view. He knew that she was capable of exaggerating the ambitions she had up her sleeve, but in this instance he was willing to give her the benefit of the doubt.

'Talk to Black Duncan,' Cordelia suggested.

'And who might Black Duncan be?' Mairi asked.

'The captain of Great Grandpa's boat,' she replied.

'Oh, that Duncan, he's nought but a rogue and he's full of seaman's fables.'

'"The sea's the very highway of content." Well, that's what Duncan told me.'

'And when did he tell you this?' her mother asked. Cordelia shrugged. 'There's not a word of truth to him and I don't want you spending time in his company.'

'The best tales have a different truth about them,' her precocious daughter replied, 'and it's not past understanding.'

Cathy sent Finlay a questioning look.

'And while he's cracking on with his tales has he ever mentioned the old music?' Mairi asked.

'Indeed he has,' the girl replied, in a tone of insult that was just perceptible. 'He told me once about an old piper on Uist who could work wonders on the imagination and one day this piper helped a panic-stricken crew avoid the rocks by playing his pipes to them. Later, when they had been rescued they all discovered that they had fallen into the same dream.'

Mairi brightened at her niece's words and asked where Duncan might be found.

'He has just taken to sea,' Cordelia said. 'I expect Great Grandpa knows where he's heading. It will be somewhere among the islands, that's for sure.'

Mairi stood still then and after glancing at her watch she rang her Grandfather. There was no reply.

'He is always early to bed so there is no point making a journey up the glen at this hour,' Cathy told her.

Mairi sat sighing and fidgeting while Cathy quizzed her daughter about Duncan. She heard the sound of her sister's words, of her surprise and horror at the amount of time Cordelia had been spending down by the docks, but thoughts of Duncan's potential were uppermost in her mind. She decided that she was too edgy to stay for supper, she needed the evening air to get the best of her thoughts, and without elaborating upon her reasons for leaving, Mairi offered a brief apology, kissed Cordelia warmly and stepped out of the house and into the garden.

The night was full of the fragrance of flowers and the foreign trees. There was no breath of wind. They were shades in some garden of dream compelled to stand and ponder for ever in an eternal night of numerous beneficent stars. No sound manifested except the lady's breathing, that to another than the dreamer would have told an old and wholesome panic story, for her bosom heaved, that breath was sweeter than the flowers. And the dryads, no whit older as they swung among the trees, still all childless, must have laughed at this revelation of an age of dream. Than that sound of maiden interest, and the far off murmur of the streams that fell seaward from woody hills, there was at first no other rumour to the ear. [4]

Andrew

Throughout his teenage years, his time at university and his first job on a newspaper, it was Andrew's ambition to possess a balance of opinions, but after three years editing a weekly newspaper column called *Opinions* the subject of balance had lost much of its meaning for him. He was bemused at first that his need of opinions could so obviously diminish, but when the weekly demand for differing viewpoints increased, just as he was growing accustomed to a decreased diet of comparative methodology, he had no option but to reflect upon his practice and no choice but to regard his presence on the *Opinions* column as a lie.

Having come to understand that the discursive approach had prevented many things from happening, Andrew decided that henceforth his approach would have a stark simplicity about it. He started this new ambition by emphasising his personal opinions in the column, but his editor quickly informed him that he was not employed for this purpose. A disaster in the making, one might think, but we should not harbour fears on Andrew's account, he is, after all, a humorous, resourceful young man who is happy to cease his prattling on and optimistic about the possibility of singing out. This sunny disposition keeps the spirit of him in such fine form that he has not felt the need to explain his poor employment prospects to his friends or family, not even to Mairi, to whom, for better or for worse, for richer, for poorer, in sickness and in health, he will soon be betrothed.

Andrew has now taken the path of direct action and his writing has blossomed into a form of play-writing that is unlikely to provide him with any kind of audience or indeed any other discernible benefit. Over the past months, plays have flown from his computer in torrents and the solace this has brought him far outweighs any of the restrictive voices he has conjured for himself in an attempt to offer some modest form of balance to his unfettered enthusiasm. His plays have no easily discernable subject matter, no characters to inspire ambition or warn of tragedy and no evidence of a space/time continuum that one could recognise. What they have in great measure is mathematics and geometry.

Each of Andrew's acts is a game of numbers and shapes on the page. The quantities he determines upon govern the amount of lines that are taken up by the speech of his characters or his stage instructions, the latter having no less importance than the former. In each act the activities that determine stage instructions and the characteristics of speech – be they monologue or dialogue – are repeated in an identical order. The number of lines either remains the same or they grow by an addition of the same number each time they are repeated. The charts that Andrew makes to create these mathematical forays are extraordinary, something that even a casual reader would find intriguing, but Andrew has no intention of publishing his schema alongside the play script. 'It's all in the music,' he tells himself, 'and if the play with numbers doesn't resonate with musicality and feeling then no amount of calculations on the page will help to create it.'

A change of noun and the increase in the number of lines are the most significant features that Andrew offers to delight us. They are a landscape of repetitive forms over which his feelings, like delicate streams upon the land's surface, flow and nourish the ground. The actions he creates have little about them that might be termed dramatic, for they more closely resemble the activity people engage in at work. His words, having little about them to suggest a search for meaning, are the expressions of everyday conversation. Without doubt, these plays, a term that may not be appropriate to them at all, are the productions of a man who has a confirmed dislike of opinion, for in the entirety of his pages there is not the slightest evidence of one, either in its hard formed aspect or in the light suppositions that often hide in its guise.

What Andrew loves most is to be busily engaged with work. That this work complies with specific rules is important. That its qualities are a confirmation that his characters are involved in a game is essential. Everything happens without preconception and the results are brim full of accident. His numerals are a foil for creating structure, the structure is a framework to support improvisation and the quotidian nature of his decision-making, if any is required, is a device for staying with what he knows. He works on, perfectly happy in the belief that if anything needs communicating it will find a way to surface and when it does it will be itself; just that.

If Andrew were to give Mairi an opportunity to read his plays it is without doubt that she would recognise the humour in them, for she is acutely attuned to the casual nature of his comedy. If his ambition is obscure and the question of its relevance is not a subject that has the potential for providing answers, then these are not issues that would deter Mairi. His essential humour is very important for our young groom, for this rare quality is the very foundation of Mairi's love for him. Typically enough, Andrew doesn't know this yet, for she has never expressed it to him, or indeed to herself, but she once told Esther that there is more to him than the sum total of his opinions in the newspaper and most of it is delightfully nutty. Esther too had suspected as much and she told Mairi that she applauded her choice of husband.

Today is an important day for Andrew. Having spent the weekend reading poems by John Ashbery, he decided in a dream last night to cease writing plays and to start writing prose. This was his first day. He continued his habit of editing words so that they filled the entire page and the intensity of his geometry as he neared the end was still the charge for him. When his last line did not take up the entire width of the page then he looked for an alternative word, sentence or layout strategy to ensure that it did. Andrew imagines that something is happening here, but he does not know what it is and this not knowing is now as important to him as the holding of balanced opinions once was during his youth and early adult years.

Alastair

Up with the lark and singing like a fine one, Alastair made his way up the Glen explaining, to an imaginary radio interviewer, the importance of having a song in one's head to accompany each day. Alastair always had a song and his family never cease to be astounded at the number and variety he can bring to mind. 'They come to me in the night,' is his excuse when they question him about them and this morning he is extolling their virtues to an invented female interviewer from the radio.

'I'm much surprised mysel' by the pertinence of the songs,' he told her, 'for they seem to gather roond the feelin's I'm having at the time and I canna guess what these things are until the song reveals 'em to me.'

It is the fishing he is out for this morning and, as he approached the stream, he changed the subject so that his imagined audience of one could hear of the pleasures of playing the great silver salmon.

For half an hour was not another word from him; he was a man bewitched, that crawled among the rushes of the bank and crouched in shadows of the boulders, and threw the lures across the linn among the playing fish, with eyes that seemed to grudge each moment that they were not on the water. [5]

Mairi, like her grandfather, is also an early riser, but on this morning she did not manage to get Alastair on the phone before his trip to the Glen. She left a message that she knew he wouldn't listen to and, without breakfast, she jumped into her car with the urgent purpose of discovering the whereabouts of Black Duncan. At Alastair's house Mairi asked his housekeeper if she knew where her grandfather could be found. 'Och, who knows,' was her reply, 'it's likely to be anywheres on that stream that you'll find 'im.' Mairi expected as much. She accepted the offer of coffee and scones from Mrs. McInnis before heading out into the landscape in search of the old fisherman.

Alastair, having located his place on the stream, was lost in thought, patiently casting his line. *For long it looked as if the fisher worked in vain; great fishes surged and leaped about his hair-lines and his feathers, but they never touched them.* 'Aren't they the frightened dirt?' Alastair declared, again addressing his imaginary interviewer. *'Not a bit of gallant spirit in them! Stop you, though!' And he fixed another lure.* [5]

Mairi moved along the bank calling Alastair's name, but not one response did she get from the angler, even though she was practically upon him. When she spied him from the brae, bent on the water-edge and whipping in the eddies where the fish lie, she ran down to him. The old man, crouched knee-deep in water, gave a twitch, turned and, just as she came nigh to him, gave her an aspect that astonished her.

All his face was puckered up with exaltation; in his eyes a curious glitter, proud and savage. 'Tha e agam, *a bhruide! – I have him, the brute!'* he screamed, and slowly backed out of the stream with his rod-point bent. Mairi *watched him, fascinated, play the fish. It threw itself in the air, and fell with great commotion in the middle of the pool, and then the line went whirling out of the wooden pirn the whole length of the pool, which ended in a shallow narrow channel.* Alastair, *with his teeth clenched and his lips drawn back from them, all in a kind of glorious agony, strained lightly on the rod and span the reel at every yard he gained upon his quarry. Repeatedly it burst away again and leaped until the pool was boiling with its fury.*

'If I had a decent stick instead of the child's playock!' said the angler in anguish. 'I never had it in my mind to touch such big ones!'

He fought with it for near an hour; at last he had it close upon the bank; they saw it rolling at their feet bluebacked, and Mairi *stretched a hand to grasp the line and lift it.*

'Put a finger upon a hair of that and there is not a timber of your body but I'll break!' roared Alastair. *'I will take him to this stone and you must tail him. Catch him by the small and grip as if it were the very bars of heaven and you by God rejected!'*

Mairi *gripped. The fish moved mightily within her hand, writhed with extraordinary power, and breaking slimy from her grasp, snapped* Alastair's *line. It slowly turned a moment, and* Alastair *with a yell dropped rod, plucked out the knife below his elbow, threw himself upon the fish, and stabbed it through the gills.*

'Sin thu!' he roared, and heaved it high upon the bank. *'Oh* Mairi*!'* he cried with brimming eyes, and, all dripping, put his arms about his granddaughter and squeezed her to his breast. He skipped then, like a child, about the fish, and fondled it like one that loved it, saying the most beautiful things in death were a child, a salmon, and a woodcock. Then broke he into a curious Gaelic brag about his prey, – he spoke of it as if it were leviathan.

'It is not so very big a fish as all that!' said Mairi, and at that the other looked again upon his prize, and his jaw fell.

'By the Books and you're right!' said he with some vexation. *'It's just a middling one, and red at that! And that is mighty droll, for I was sure this moment that he was a monster, and the side of him like a silver ship. But I think you'll must agree I played him pretty!* With two slashes of the small black knife he ripped the ends from off the salmon, and he shoved its middle, wrapped with ferns, into his knapsack. [5]

'I need to find Black Duncan,' Mairi told him, 'and I'm informed that he's away on your business.'

'Not mine,' Alastair declared. 'It's your great-uncle Donald as has him oot and if I know Donald there's a secret in the proceedings that he won't be the quickest in the land to explain to ye.'

As they walked back together Alastair started singing.
*Gone fishin', by a shady wady pool,
I'm wishin', I could be that kind of fool.*
Then, thinking Mairi was the young female interviewer from the radio, he explained the importance of the song.

Christine

Jean-Paul placed the ladder against the wall under Christine's window, the dog barked and his heart thumped. The risks of this adventure were greater than anything he had undertaken before. One half of him wished that Christine would change her mind and the other half was in a dream. *The bushes were big masses of shade; the trees, a little more remote, seemed to watch him with an irony that made him half ashamed. What an appalling night! Over him came the sentiments of the robber, the marauder, the murderer. As he held the lantern on his finger a faint wind swung it, and its lances of light danced rhythmic through the gloom. He put it under his plaid, and prepared to give the signal whistle. For the life of him he could not give it utterance; his lips seemed to have frozen, not with fear, for he was calm in that way, but with some commingling of emotions where fear was not at all. When he gave breath to his hesitating lips, it went through inaudible.*

What he might have done then may only be guessed, for the opening of the window overhead brought an end to his hesitation.[6]

'Is it you?' Jean-Paul looked up to the place where Christine's anxious whisper came from and, wetting his lips with his tongue, he whispered loudly that the ladder was in place. 'Give me some light,' Christine asked.

'I dare not,' our hero replied. Christine threw her bag down in an attempt to hit him.

'Am I to do the daring and break my neck perhaps?'

Out flashed the lantern from beneath his plaid and he held it up to the window. Christine *leant over and all his hesitation fled. He had never seen her more alluring. Her hair had become somehow unfastened, and, without untidiness, there lay a lock across her brow; all her blood was in her face, her eyes might indeed have been the flames he had fancied, for to the appeal of the lantern they flashed back from great and rolling depths of luminousness. Her lips seemed to have gathered up in sleep the wealth of a day of kissing. A screen of tartan that she had placed about her shoulders had slipped aside in her movement at the window and showed her neck, ivory pale and pulsing.* [6]

The second Christine's foot reached the ground Jean-Paul turned off the lantern, placed the ladder on the ground, lifted her bag and made for the gate. Christine remained standing on the spot where she had landed. Having lived in a world of romance since she was ten, Christine had imagined a very different scene of elopement to this one. Jean-Paul turned to her and motioned frantically with his arm that she should follow him.

'So we're just going to run off then?' she asked with more than a hint that something else should happen.

'Yes, what are you waiting for?'

'Well they don't just run off in the movies.'

'This isn't a movie, Christine.' He ran to her, kissed her quickly and took her arm.

'Well it seems to me,' the girl complained, pulling back her arm, 'that you're not making the most of it. You could at least be a little more cheerful.'

Jean-Paul looked anxiously between his sweetheart and the house, hoping that one or the other would move and give him a reason for action. The adrenaline was running fast in him and his only possibilities were fight or flight. Christine stood, her arms folded, her lips pouting and her eyes glaring at the hasty cavalier. The dog barked.

'Do you love me?' Christine asked.

'Of course I do, but if you want to come with us you had better come now. The others are waiting in the car. Come on.'

Christine shivered and coughed. The early morning was cold and heavy with dew. Jean-Paul, crouching slightly, looked about nervously. He was still ready for action.

'I didn't just sell out to the first guy who offered to take me you know.'

'Well I certainly admire your honesty. It's really important at a time like this.'

'I could still go to Scotland with Papa.'

Jean-Paul was disinclined to engage in the argument. She had pleaded with him to take her on holiday and now that the rain had started he couldn't see any point in waiting. He dropped her case with a thump on the path and glowered at her. 'Now or never,' he said.

'Never,' she said and she immediately regretted it.

Jean-Paul darted away and reached the waiting car

before Christine had moved a muscle. It was her tear ducts that operated first, followed quickly by all the functions required of a body to sustain disconsolate sobbing. She half realised that they might be sobs of relief, but it was the half of her that throbbed with embarrassment that hurt her the most.

The reaction of her friends was everything to Christine and her only option for saving face now was to blame Jean-Paul for his gauche nervousness, but it was simply not in her to do this.

It was the cold in the air that put a stop to it, this and the realisation that she needed her father on her side now; a condition that would be impossible if he found her in the front garden at this hour with her bag packed. She lifted the ladder to an upright position directly below her window and, taking up her bag, she climbed back to her bedroom. It was with some anger that she pushed the ladder back into the garden.

At breakfast, having earlier returned the ladder to the garage, she talked with great interest about their impending trip to Scotland and her father wondered what might have caused this sudden enthusiasm in her. Until then she had been disparaging about the visit.

Her older brother, Sebastian was similarly perplexed by her sudden change of heart, but unlike his father he couldn't resist taking up the issue.

'I bet you've broken up with your boyfriend,' he teased, but Christine did not respond. She placed her hand on her father's arm and addressed him affectionately.

'Don't worry Papa, whatever he says, I'm with you.'

Ethan

The twins, Ethan and Esther, agreed that they should not study at the same university. They were both attracted to the subjects of architecture and fine art, but neither could decide which one to choose, so Esther applied for fine art, Ethan for architecture, and both agreed that they would change places at a later time if decisions dictated that they should take the opposite course.

Esther had her hair cut short to increase her likeness to Ethan and they used the same photograph of Ethan on their application forms. They gave the same address and the same mobile phone number and they scrawled illegibly the letters of their first names. They made no comment when the university spelt them incorrectly.

As it happened they did switch places, Esther to study architecture and Ethan to study fine art. The respective administration departments never learned of their switch, never suspected trickery from them of any kind, and later, when they occasionally attended a lecture meant for the other twin, the academic staff were never aware it.

Esther approached architecture like a sculptor and on completing her studies she set up business as an interior designer. What attracted the clients to her was her peculiar way of creating furniture, just that, and the way she placed her objects in particular locations. Having an intense interest in the way people inhabit space, Esther established a radical way of expressing it. Recently, when designing an apartment for a client, she demolished the hallway and placed a kitchen counter across the entrance, the reverse side out, transforming everyone who entered into the cook. She loved it most when small decisions had a major impact.

At college Ethan made sculpture as a bookmaker makes books and now that his yearning for narrative cannot be placated in any other way he concentrates exclusively on writing. Very little had come of his efforts, but he is content to be slow in promoting himself, unlike his method of writing, which he does at break-neck speed. A colleague of his, after sitting next to him one morning, complained that the speed of his typing had given him a nervous twitch in the left eye. Ethan, thinking this was more likely caused by the noise his fingers made on the keys, offered to upgrade his keyboard.

Ethan spent the whole of his first day in Inverness at the hotel reading Neil Munro's *Fancy Farm* and the next morning, having finished it, he went to the library hoping to borrow another book by Scotland's famous son. He was shocked that there was not one copy to be had, but after diving into the nearest computer he found copies of *Children Of Tempest* and *The Daft Days* for sale. He ordered both, but was deeply perturbed about waiting 'til his arrival home before he could read them. As he was leaving he told the librarian that he would die if he could not find more Munro to read soon.

'You should go to Leakey's,' the librarian informed him, 'the second-hand bookshop, down the way.'

Ethan sprang out of the library, down Church Street and into Greyfriars Hall, an old Gaelic Church filled with books. He asked a fellow presiding at a desk if there was any Neil Munro to be had and within minutes he was sitting on the floor with each of Munro's novels before him. Then, with the books placed in piles between his legs to prevent anyone else making a bid for them, Ethan read the opening paragraph of every novel. *John Splendid, The New Road, The Daft Days, The Shoes Of Fortune, Fancy Farm, Doom Castle, Children Of Tempest, Gilian The Dreamer*, all of them until he came at last to the short stories, *The Lost Pibroch, Jaunty Jock* and *Ayrshire Idylls*. He started on *The Lost Pibroch*.

To the make of a piper go seven years of his own learning and seven generations before. If it is in, it will out, as the Gaelic old-word says; if not, let him take to the net or sword. At the end of his seven years one born to it will stand at the start of knowledge, and leaning a fond ear to the drone, he may have parley with old folks of old affairs. Playing his tune of the 'Fairy Harp', he can hear his forefolks, plaided in skins, towsy-headed and terrible, grunting at the oars and snoring in the caves; he has his whittle and club in the 'Desperate Battle' (my own tune, my darling!), where the white haired sea-rovers are on the shore, and a stain's on the edge of the tide; or, trying his art on Laments, he can stand by the cairn of kings, ken the colour of Fingal's hair, and see the moon-glint on the hook of the Druids![7]

'What sort of heart do I have if I don't buy them all?' Ethan asked himself, and he carried the whole set to the counter. The fellow there showed no surprise as he placed his hoard on the desk, but upon seeing the author he shouted, '*Slochd-a-chubair gu bragh*!' – which is the rallying cry of the Inneraora burghers – 'the man's a *taibhsear.*' Our young writer stared at him. 'The man's a visionary, d'ye ken?' Ethan nodded uncertainly, 'one with second-sight,' the bookseller reiterated.

Ethan didn't take in what the man said, he was too anxious lest someone should accuse him of making off with a complete set of the nation's treasures, but once the books were in his possession and he was out of Leakey's his senses returned to him. He made his way in the rain, the two great carrier bags weighing heavily on him, and he offered a little joyful thanks to whoever it was who was responsible for his fate on this day. Later he relieved himself of the weight of the books by purchasing a suitcase with wheels from the covered market.

When Ethan entered Esther's hotel room, she was lying across the suitcases reading Mairi's copy of *Fancy Farm*. It was past eleven, the time when they should have vacated the room; the time when they should already be on the train travelling westwards, but Esther made no mention of the fact. Ethan unzipped his case and took out one book after another. 'There is still the biography, his memoirs and the *Para Handy* stories to buy,' he told her, 'but these should keep us busy 'til we return.'

Esther kissed her book, smiled knowingly at her brother and eagerly inspected his great hoard of books.

Donald

From the beginning Donald was never one to control his passions and to see him now, a man in his withered eighties, you might believe him to be the sole survivor of that old breed of highlander who hunted in the forests, slept in the heather and could name every ghost that haunted the glens. It was in his forties that Donald had the old savage awakened in him. Some say it was an odd relapse, others that it was his hour of glory, but either way he has lived with its consequences happily enough.

When his brother Alastair inherited the family home it was understood that Donald should have the old family plot in Kilree along with the pile of stones that was once a mansion. It was a quirk of errant bureaucracy that caused this rocky outcrop to be included in a sale of land that stretched from Cairn Dearg to Carsaig, but once Donald learned of his disinheritance and then understood that the new owner's rights were protected by law, he took it upon himself to return to the old ways of settling differences. He dressed himself in his tartan, cleaned an old musket and, with a claymore sword at his haunch, stepped out for that cleft in the mountain where the river joins the sea, the place that was the land of his fathers, with the sole intention of reclaiming it.

It was many years before the new owners gleaned that Donald had taken back his old estate and by then he was joined by a significant band of folk, the tales of his enterprise having spread far and wide. The folk were mostly squatters and they, together with Donald, fixed the fences, repaired the main house, occupied the outhouses and cleared land for the parking of their many vans, trailers and caravans. They grew crops in small terraces, had livestock neatly penned and were without fear of the owner, who, to their great good fortune, never lifted a finger to remove them from his property.

The first thing a man to-day would do in the like circumstances would be to call for the police; but even today in the Islands, the police are rare and remote from Kilree, and at that time it was as ill to reach them as to reach St Kilda, even if there had been no popular conviction that the civil law alone is all that a Highland gentleman can with propriety call into action. [8]

It had been many years since Mairi had visited her great-uncle Donald, but if she was to learn about Black Duncan's voyage a visit to him now was essential; he had no phone at the place. She knew there were fewer folk at the mansion these days, but as she drew near she was surprised to see but one window shining in the gloaming. *The silvery fog which often filled the valley where the mansion lay, austere and old and lonely, gave to the natural dusk a quality of dream, an air of vague estrangement, a brooding and expectant sentiment. The trees stood round like shining ghosts, and evening birds were mourning in the clammy thickets.* [9]

Mairi beat upon the knocker and as its clangour rang through the dark interior it was trepidation she felt. Of this, of course, there was little need, for when Donald opened the door he gave her enough delighted welcome to make her feel the honoured guest. He invited Mairi to sit by his hearth, fed her cakes and whisky and the pair of them blethered of old and new times for many an hour. In the main Donald's memory proved to be in good working order, but there were odd inconsistencies about him. When Mairi reminded him of her coming wedding he expressed some surprise that it was still the custom for young folk to get married and when she asked him where Black Duncan had taken the boat he could only eulogize upon the man's character and upon that of his friend Hurricane Jack.

Duncan, he claimed, *iss a man that can sail anything and go anywhere, and always the perfect chentleman. A millionaire's yat or a washing boyne – it's aal the same to him.*'

Before long Mairi understood that it was on Jack's account that Donald had employed Duncan, but he would never give Mairi the reason, he would only talk on about his friend. *Jeck is wan man in a hundred, and ass good ass two if there was anything in the way of trouble, for man! he's strong, strong! He has a back on him like a shipping-box, and when he will come down Tarbert quay on a Friday night after a good fishing, and the trawlers are arguing, it's two yerds to the step with him and a bash in the side of his hat for fair defiance. But he never hit a man twice, for he's aye the perfect chentleman iss*

Hurricane Jeck. Of course, you must understand, he wass not known as Hurricane Jeck till the time I'm going to tell you of, when he stole the sheep. [10]

Donald never got round to telling Mairi about the sheep, but she guessed that the reason for Duncan's voyage was to transport Jack to a hiding place in far off Islands. Mairi tried everything to learn of Duncan's destination, but it was past midnight before Donald finally conceded that all he knew of the whereabouts of Duncan was that he was to collect Jack from Castle Quair, the place where his friend Murdo was providing shelter.

Having spent a harsh night with rough blankets on a makeshift bed, Mairi rose early in the morn's morn, for Castle Quair was nearly a day's journey from Kilree. She arranged for a fellow called Urquhart to drive her great-uncle to his brother's house in time for the wedding and as she travelled south she tried to recall if she had ever met Murdo Macaskill, the tenant of Castle Quair. The place itself she had not visited, but she knew of its location in the sea and prayed that the tides would be in her favour.

It was late when Mairi stood gazing at the majestic scene with the romantic fortress at its centre and to her great relief the tide was out and a series of wooden platforms were placed across the muddy foreshore to the castle. She was making for the steps leading to the platforms when she saw a young fellow, who was already upon them, slip and fall to the bottom. She ran to him and when she was close by he lifted his head and she recognised the man as Andrew's dear friend, Clyde. 'What a surprise,' she said and Clyde stared up at her, a broad smile upon his face.

Aileen

After a series of text messages between Esther, Mairi and Cathy, it was agreed that Finlay would meet Ethan and Esther at the railway station and drive them to his mother-in-law's house where they were to stay. Esther had known Mairi long enough not to be surprised or indeed offended by her friend's disappearance, but Aileen, Mairi's mother was endlessly apologetic about her daughter's absence.

'I hope Andrew will exercise some discipline with her once they're married,' she told them reprovingly, 'but at present he is *so daft about her, she could lead him round the country with a cobweb, – that's the way with men before ye marry them.'* [11]

Aileen, being an excellent cook, prepared a fine supper and she invited Cathy, Finlay and Cordelia over to join her guests. Aileen, a housekeeper-in-chief, loved the role of hostess and she cared deeply about the intricacies of good social behaviour. Her most pleasurable task was the orchestration of conversation, a task that she carried out with an ear that was marvellously tuned to pick up on boredom, but on this occasion she realised that there were complexities to this role that she was not prepared for. Finlay, Ethan, Cathy and Esther were overly taken up with their exclusive conversations and this had upset her, so, in a manner that indicated her disdain for being left out, Aileen sauntered across to the window, lifted it wide open and addressed her guests.

'I wonder what you think of my paintings?' she asked and her assembled guests ceased their conversation and stared, first at Aileen and then at her paintings. Cordelia, looking up from drawings that covered the entire surface of a napkin, smiled at her grandmother.

'Oh mother, your paintings can hardly be talked about as one might consider art,' Cathy complained. 'The folk in them are your ancestors. This maybe a virtue in our family, but it doesn't warrant an opinion on them from the world at large.'

'Well our guests, being artists, might offer an opinion,' Aileen retorted. 'There's hardly a better way to get to know a person than to hear their view of painting.'

'It's not easy to talk of painting,' Ethan offered, 'even for an artist. I think one should spend time with them before offering an opinion. It's the reason you have them that's important. If they mean something to you then they are beautiful.'

'Good for you, young man,' Aileen told him, 'but it remains a pleasant thing to hear talk of them. You will have guessed no doubt that I did not buy them as a job lot and you might assume that I have no particular desire for an assortment of military portraits, no matter how cheerful the hues might be, the question for me is this; can you feel the presence of war behind them? They were painted to celebrate the return of my great-grandfather and the loss of his brother in the war.'

'Mother,' Cathy exclaimed in a voice that expressed her exasperation, 'how can you imagine that your guests might feel the presence of a war that has long been forgotten, just because it's painted?'

At this Aileen, with dignity and a slight huff of impatience about her, left the room and Cathy was left considering what show of contrition she must now offer her mother. Aileen, having enjoyed her show of defiance, returned soon enough, a broad smile upon her countenance and a large bowl of trifle in her hands. She placed the bowl on the table and proceeded to serve her guests. Cordelia addressed her.

'When you left, *the room all at once seemed to fill with the trampling of men and the shrilling of pipers, with ships, quays, tumultuous towns, camps, and all the wonders of the shepherd's battle stories round the fire, and your great-grandfather was in a field, and it was the afternoon with a blood-red sky beyond the fir-trees, dense smoke floating across it and the cries of men cutting each other down ... I saw the stiff figure of a fallen man in a high collar like the man portrayed upon the wall, and his hand was still in the hilt of a reddened sword and about him were the people he had slain.*'[12]

Cordelia was standing in the middle of the floor feeling much older than she had done that morning. The adults gazed at her. Her nostrils had expanded, her eyes glistened and the sound of her quickened breath filled the room. Aileen gestured for her granddaughter to come to her chair and, drawing the girl to her in an embrace, she attempted to relieve her embarrassment.

'What is it?' she asked in the Gaelic; the language she used when a moment of special fondness was called for.

'I don't know,' Cordelia replied. 'I was just thinking of what you said about feeling the war and then I saw all those men who did not come home again.'

'Goodness child,' Aileen exclaimed, 'you have your great-grandfather, Alastair's imagination about you,' and turning the girl's head to the side she whispered in her ear. 'That's why you and I get along so nicely, isn't it?'

Cordelia nodded and wiped away a tear. She was amazed that her grandmother understood her. Grown-ups rarely did. Her dreams, her fancies, her *spectacles of the inner eye were things that she had grown ashamed of. But here was a shrewd little lady who seemed to think her fancy and confidence nothing discreditable.* [12]

Until this moment Cordelia believed that she could only talk to her angel when she was in need of some comfort. It was only her angel that understood Cordelia's *vagrant mind, so sometimes in passionate outbursts, when the words ran over the heels of each other, sometimes in shrinking, stammering, reluctant sentences she told her how the seasons affected her, and the morning and the night, the smells of things, the sounds of woods and the splash of waters, and the mists streaming along the ravines. She told her – or rather she made her understand, for her language was simple – how at sudden outer influences her whole being fired, and from so trivial a thing as a cast-off horseshoe on the highway she was compelled to picture the rider, and set him upon the saddle and go riding with him to the King of Erin's court.* [12]

Murdo

On the night he arrived at Quair Castle, Clyde was warmly welcomed, given a bed for the night and invited to the party that Murdo Macaskill was holding that evening to celebrate his sixtieth birthday. Clyde understood very little of what was said to him, but he felt nicely entertained by Murdo and his guests. He was impressed by the timeless life they led here and he felt honoured to be in a place that showed so little evidence of strife.

The next morning Clyde was lying still, trying to recall the past evening's events, but he couldn't even remember how he got to his bed and for this he blamed the great quantity of drink he had consumed. The only thing he could bring to mind was a tune and while he dressed he whistled it to himself. Downstairs, as he stepped into the hall, he remembered that he had asked a piper to whistle this tune to him many times over and as he entered the kitchen it seemed to resonate through his body as though his bones knew it. He was wondering how this could be so when Murdo greeted him heartily.

'Gude mornin'. You're early on the move. I hope ye sleepit weel; it was a gowsty night, was it not?'

'Oh, too much whisky, I think,' Clyde replied with a broad but sheepish grin.

'Aye, aye, and you'd best ca canny wi' the drink my laddie, specially as you're aboot to be mairied an all.'

'What!' Clyde exclaimed, 'not I. It's my friend's wedding I'm going to, not mine.'

'Och! Then you must have reckoned we were half oot o' our wits, for we had the other notion aboot it. I wondered why ye were in such an awful hurry when the ring was no' bought yet. So and on, and I'm glad for ye to remain single yet. The maist deleeberate mairriage maun be aye a lottery and I was sick to think of ye starting on such a mischancy thing with too much haste aboot it. I've known folks gang heels-over-hurdies on findin' a partner and then get in an awfu' swither 'cos they havena clue what might guide 'em on. But I'm sorry if we said the wrong things to ye, laddie.'

'Well, to tell the truth I didn't understand too much of what was said,' Clyde told him and his host gave out a jocular laugh and slapped him on the back.

'And ye'll be none the worse for that,' Murdo said. 'Eat some breakfast and I'll phone the gairige and have 'em tak' ye to yon car and if they canna feex it straight off then you'll be welcome to stay as long as you weesh.'

Clyde was grateful for the offer, but later, when the mechanic told him that his car would take days to repair, he was even more grateful. It was as he was returning to the castle to inform Murdo of the turn of events that he took his tumble down the steps; Mairi came running towards him, calling out to know if he was injured.

As Clyde recognised her, he replied to her concern for his bones with a smile and the assurance that he didn't mind accomplishing his descent quicker than intended.

'What are we going to do with you?' she laughed.

They stood for some time on the foreshore talking about how they had come to be at Castle Quair and when Mairi explained her mission to find Black Duncan, Clyde, excited by the tale, pleaded to be allowed to accompany her. Mairi was surprised by this request but before long she felt comforted at the thought of having Clyde by her side. It was a gay step that they took along the platforms to talk with the tenant of Castle Quair.

Murdo was delighted to see them and he remembered meeting Mairi before at her grandfather's house. After pouring his guests a dram, he listened to Mairi's tale about her need of Black Duncan who knew a piper who could charm the spirits.

'D'ye know where Duncan can be found?' she asked.

'I dinna know it chile,' he told her. 'He was no here long enough to learn it. He rowed to the castle and straight way took Hurricane Jack to the Islands. I'm tell't by Jack that it's Loch Boisdale they're heading for first, but I canna tell more.' Mairi stood silent, a picture of disappointment. '*Mo chreach*, it's not all lost yet lass,' he insisted, 'but if you want yon Duncan you'd best be off to Oban early o' the morn's morn or you'll miss the Uist ferry.' Mairi raised a smile. 'And as you'll be needin' an early night you're maist welcome t' a bed here.'

'Thank you, Murdo, you're the very thing.'

'Och, it's nae so much. Wi' a place this size, hospitality's the best thing for it. Why, if we had just the peats, we had a *céilidh*,' and he offered them both another dram.

Clyde declined, with the excuse that he was still nursing a sore head, and he returned to his room.

'*Tha'm fear so air falbh*!' Murdo said after Clyde had left and seeing the incomprehensible expression on Mairi, he gave her the English for it. 'The man's away wi' it!

'But he's so kind and joco Murdo. Andrew, my soon to be husband, is very fond of him.'

'What, and is it you who's to be mairied then?' Murdo asked, and upon learning that it was he danced a little jig before suddenly stopping, wearing a most serious look.

'So it's your weddin' the laddie's up for? Och, the very sound o't maks my heid sair,' and he scratched his scalp as he reflected upon Mairi's news.

'What is it?' Mairi asked.

'*Faoinsgeulachd*! Such emptiness and folly,' he added in the English. 'I'd best let ye ken the outs and ins o' the fun we were havin' wi' our stranger last night,' and he stopped to shake his head. 'The laddie arrived wi' a bawbee frown upon his countenance, so we took 'im in. We asked where he was headin' and understood that he was in a great hurry to be mairied. Then, in a kindly way, d'ya ken, some folk started on singing, *Now That She's Heavy* and whistlin' *Too Long In This Condition,* you'll know the tunes I'm on about. It were jist a bit wee joke between us with no harm meant and I know for a fact that the young laddie didna' ken a thing of our meaning.'

Mairi smiled and the two of them gave in to laughter while Murdo again whistled the teasing tune.

'He's a prize fellow,' Mairi said, 'and don't worry, there's not a one anywhere that can resist teasing him.'

James

Andrew, travelling to Scotland by train with James, was taking the opportunity to explain to his brother the radical shift he had taken and his decision to move away from journalism. James listened attentively, but he needed little elaboration on the theme to comprehend his brother's position, for his own decision to take up the publishing of poetry had been made for similar reasons. Not wishing to dwell on the subject of his brother's employment difficulties longer than was necessary, James expressed his eagerness to read Andrew's recent writing. Andrew opened his lap top, selected a page of prose and handed it to his brother to read.

'No one is waiting around now; the new transformation has started and everyone is beginning to feel the warm glow that accompanies branching out. The terms prevalent in the days of disenchanted bureaucracy have disappeared, along with its advocates, and it has become clear that with every expelled breath healing occurs; the fractured debris of over consumption is being remoulded; spontaneity is being fertilised and silver linings are being generated where none could have been imagined before. It was the mass of contradictions that held everyone frozen for so long, but now that we have broken through, now that a little light is just visible in the dank fog, young and old alike are beginning to sense their way through the confusion.

'There is nothing specific to be done, only some growing that is necessary, only an acceptance that we must submit to, a listening to the rhythm of growth and the eager assumption that we hear through our bones as well as our ears. Having first learned how to delight in generous instincts it has become acutely obvious that the old way of judging has proved itself worthless. New loves are born without the need to eschew the old loves and the beliefs in life by fear, immobility without contract and the primacy of the law have been elbowed out, leaving no more than a handful of solicitors whose job it is to practice positive minimalism and oversee the decline of continual interference.

'Everyone now works at expanding magnanimous attention, so that nothing of the new unfolding is missed and we can attend wholeheartedly to the unlearning and fall more regularly into each other. Each new day is lived like a life-span. The change is not without stumbling or self consciousness, but gradually, as the habit of fear for predicting risk is replaced by benign casualness, the carefree buzz more assuredly hums. It confirms humanity's rich enjoyment of comedy and affirms its collective certainty that anything is only worth the candle if playfulness is its starting point.'

'Well if this isn't packed with opinion I don't know what is,' James said at the reading's conclusion.

Andrew was taken aback by the response, but when he

saw the smile of pleasure on his brother's face he knew that his writing had fulfilled its task.

'Its poetry sure enough,' James declared, 'and I want to read everything you've written. Now I am going to show you something', and he handed his brother a book. 'This is Scotland's first modern poet, circa 1898.'

Now we were in a tract of country mournful beyond my poor description. I know corries in Argile that whisper silken to the winds with juicy grasses, corries where the deer love to prance deep in the cool dew, and the beasts of far-off woods come in bands at their seasons and together rejoice. I have seen the hunter in them and the shepherd too, coarse men in life and occupation, come sudden among the blowing rush and whispering reed, among the bog-flower and the cannoch, unheeding the moor-hen and the cailzie-cock rising, or the stag of ten at pause, while they stood, passionate adventurers in a rapture of the mind, held as it were by the spirit of such places as they lay in a sloeberry bloom of haze, the spirit of old good songs, the baffling surmise of the piper and the bard. To those corries of my native place will be coming in the yellow moon of brock and foumart – the beasts that dote on the autumn eves – the People of Quietness; have I not seen their lanthorns and heard their laughter in the night? – so that they must be blessed corries, so endowed since the days when the gods dwelt in them without tartan and spear in the years of the peace that had no beginning. [13]

Andrew was stunned. He sat quietly, breathing in the cool elegiac smoothness of the Scottish poet and though he was filled with curiosity about the author he wanted to ask no questions of him. He read the text again, this time consciously swimming in the sense of each word, the feelings evoked by the language and the enjoyable uncertainty that lay between its classic simplicity and its modern complexity. He read it a third time and only then did he speak.

'He allows us to come to him from such a distance,' Andrew declared. 'He doesn't demand understanding, he rather invites us to merge that space between our yearning and our uncertainty and then he aerates the space as though he were responsible for nourishing our soil.'

'It's his orchestration,' James says. 'His orchestration of minutiae is superb and we are so engrossed with descriptions like, *coming sudden among the blowing rush and whispering reed, among the bog-flower and the cannoch,* that all else before us is forgotten. He reduces our awareness, fixes us on the pleasant passing of time and then gently introduces us to *the People of Quietness, who lived in the years of the peace that had no beginning.* Suddenly we are aware that the earth has shifted on its axis. Nothing is the same, for his words have done something to increase the moon's gravitational pull. Then, lest we become concerned about how we might take our first steps in this new place, he moves us briskly back to our journey through the landscape and invites us again to continue dancing. Oh how I wish that everything could be as mysterious as this, as mysterious as the place that you also give us, where everyone is entreated to develop the expanding possibilities of magnanimous attention.'

Duncan

When Mairi and Clyde stood together on the deck of 'The Princess Louise', entranced as the peaks of Hecla and Benmore came into view, Mairi reflected upon Clyde. She had never spent much time with him and without doing so she would never have guessed that a fellow who had cracked his skull on a low bulkhead and tripped numerous times over ropes and raised thresholds could be such truly fine company. Even in the thick of sea sickness he had behaved as if the state of being green, black and blue suited him as well as anyone who, having a rosy flush about their cheeks, was out walking on a warm bright morning. She decided that the world was simply alive with possibility for Clyde and as the passing landscape displayed its colourful detail, joy simply flowed from him – it was clear that he could hardly believe that he was anywhere but among the fairy isles. It was as if the voice and memory of them spoke of a golden age of sunshine and eternal spring, as if he had recently come from realms of morning freshness where the sun was always in the sky and only the finest breezes could blow on him.

Mairi, having previously sent a text to Cordelia asking where Duncan could be found if he were in Loch Boisdale, received her reply; 'The Black Whale Inn at the foot of the quay,' were Cordelia's words. For this reason Mairi and Clyde spent the afternoon at the Inn surrounded by a good many raucous mariners. Duncan appeared at six. He was not in the least surprised that his employer's granddaughter was seated there and he escorted them to The Skipper's Room and called to the landlord to bring them ale. Mairi soon told Duncan that she had learned from her niece that he knew a piper who was perfect at the pibroch and then she explained why it was so important that he play at her wedding.

'Och, but I were tellin' her aboot the Lost *Piobaireachd*,' Duncan replied, 'and this is the *Piobaireachd* of goodbyes. It'll no do ye for a weddin' *It is the tune of broken clans, that sets the men on a foray and makes cold hearthstones. It was played in Glenshira when Gilleasbuig Gruamach could stretch stout swordsmen from Boshang to Ben Bhuidhe, and where are the folks of Glenshira this day? I saw a cheery night in Carnus that's over Lochow, and song and story busy about the fire, and the Moidart man played it for a wager. In the morning the weans were without fathers, and Carnus men were scattered about the wide world.*[14] It's the charmed pipes ye'll be after and I know of only ane man on this island who can play 'em, a man by the name of Craig who lives out in Corodale, but I'll not be botherin' 'im wi' this request, for it's certain that he'll no play at a weddin'. The quiet and solitary hilltop is the place for him these days and it's rare for 'im to bring folk together to *céilidh*.'

'What's a kailey?' Clyde asked.

'It's sitting by peat fires in groups to make entertainment,'

Duncan told him. *'Tales ancient and heroic, of Fingal the Brave and Ossian the plucker of harps, are told; songs of sea and pasture-land, and short love and long war, are sung: guesses are put and repartee abounds. Sometimes too, a gifted man will fill a sheepskin with a gush of pride and squeeze the most marvellous tunes from reeds and drones, expressing, to all who have the ears to hear, the ecstasy that lies in remembrance and regret, till the folk lean forward on their seats, and with blood-red faces look into the peat-flame and the ember, something with no words for its description, something old and melancholy and unrecoverable stirring them to tears.'* [15]

Mairi was certain that Craig was her last hope, so she relentlessly pressed the old mariner to take her to the piper and after a few more ales her efforts were rewarded.

The next morning they were on a road that crosses *the pleasant sandy plains facing the Atlantic that turn and bask in the bosom of the world, murmuring a little in the creeks, and showing a curl of grey on the distant Monach Isles. The road soon left the shore and brought them into the country of the lochs, past dark and thoughtful barps knee-deep in the rushy tarns, past ruined duns where ravens pecked in the eyeless gables – old strongholds of the tribes, remembering. Beyond Askernish and Mingary, Ollay Loch and Ormaclett Castle, and then through grave Glen Dorochay, seeking the Pass of Hellisdale that comes out upon the east of Uist.* [16] *A bleak land it might seem to them that have no inward fires, and yet a land most brave, often most beautiful, acceptable to God, and edifying extremely. On the edge of Kinavreck a piper stood who knew it so, and threw his instrument into his arm, and, full of pride and happiness, charmed the uproarious sea with mountain songs.* [17]

'That's no your man,' Duncan told them as they stood, astonished by the sound, 'that's young Coll, his son, but we must wait a whiles by yon croft for his return, for he'll no be pleased if we enter his faither's place wi'oot 'im.'

Mairi declared that he sounded fine and asked what he was playing. Duncan, with his head areel to the fine tripling, told her that he was laying the ground of *Bodaich nam Briogais*. Clyde's hands moved gently through the air. Never in his life had he been as quiet as he was then.

When young Coll returned he greeted the strangers and invited them into his small bothy with its turf walls and absence of windows. He introduced them to Craig, his father, who was sitting at the fire winding pirns for the weaver-folks. Mairi went across to him to shake his hand and she realised then by the movement of the old man's hand that he was blind.

'You'll eat the stranger's bite and lip the stranger's cup?' Craig asked and Clyde, looking nervously at Mairi, nodded his head. 'And can ye only nod a fair heed at an inviteetion?' the old man enquired of him. Clyde nodded again and timidly asked how he knew of his fair head. 'Your tongue tells,' Craig said. '*A fair man has aye a soft bit in his speech, like the lapping of milk in a cogie; and a black one, like your friend there, has the sharp ring of a thin burn in frost running into an iron pot.*' [18]

The lean old man stood to his shanks, lifted his pipes, filled the bag at a breath and a big drone filled the rafters.

Cathy

'Would you care for another whisky?' Finlay asked; an invitation that Ethan accepted and Esther declined, claiming that the first had gone to her head. Cathy entered from the kitchen, handed her empty glass to Finlay, removed her apron, threw it over the back of a dining chair and pressed play on the CD player. A burst of bagpipes from a military band filled the room and Finlay moved quickly to turn the sound down before turning it off. Cathy's mobile chirped, indicating a text message.

'Mairi has found Black Duncan and she and Clyde are visiting a piper. She'll be back directly if he agrees to play at the wedding. We must quickly progress her book, but we cannot write the portraits as the guests who have responded to our request for profiles are too few.'

Her guests knew nothing of the subject she referred to and Finlay, recognising this, explained her idea of making a book as a present for the married couple.

'Can't you write the portraits yourself?' Esther asked.

'Well Finlay is actually doing the writing and he doesn't know the half of them.'

'We could fill you in on the friends if you could do the family,' Esther offered.

Cathy pondered this. 'What about the photographs? Andrew's brother James is a photographer and he has agreed to come up early to take shots of the family, but we still need photographs of the friends.'

'James is a publisher, not a photographer,' Esther informed her hostess.

'Oh how difficult,' Cathy moaned. 'I'm sure I was told otherwise. Maybe we could forget about photographs.'

'Good idea,' said Finlay, 'without images we could emphasize the fictional, lyrical qualities of everyone. I could even donate some characters from my novel...' He stopped and checked himself, realising what, in his enthusiasm, he had just offered.

'Are you calling it a novel now?' Cathy asked, just as Ethan offered the news that he too was writing a novel. The two men eyed each other suspiciously for a moment.

'Ethan has been writing furiously, ever since he read Neil Munro on the train up.' Esther explained. 'He is borrowing great swathes of the author's texts and Munro's descriptions of the landscape would add nicely to your subject. Why don't you both share your material?'

The two men again eyed each other with suspicion and both made a gesture with their shoulders to indicate their willingness, in a rather noncommittal and uncertain way.

'Surely you can't just borrow great swathes of another author's text,' Cathy advised, 'its plagiarism.'

'Not so,' Esther replied. 'It's only plagiarism if you present the work as your own.'

'Well it's infringement of copyright then,' Cathy countered. 'If Ethan wants to publish this work he will have to get permission from the copyright holder.'

'Well I doubt that Mairi's wedding book is going to find a publisher is it,' Esther remarked.

'Well if James is a publisher it might.'

They all gazed at Cathy. With this comment Esther quickly changed her original estimation of her hostess.

Finlay addressed Ethan. 'We deal with the crisis of authenticity all the time don't we? Art connects with previous art; we all have to find our position.'

'The anxiety of influence,' Ethan offered, and added, 'Harold Bloom,' to reference his quotation. After a smile of recognition from Finlay, Ethan said, 'I don't have a moral position on it. As far as I'm aware I write without knowledge or forethought. If I was driving over a Scottish moor and mud and grass became attached to my car, I can't be accused of stealing the stuff, for I didn't choose what stuck to it. And if I decided to sell the car without cleaning it, or without editing the content, I wouldn't have to credit the Highlands Authority first would I?'

Cathy tutted. 'You may be too clever by half, Ethan, and too fast for your own good. You can't arrive in Scotland one day and leave with our literary heritage the next.'

'He's not making off with it,' said Esther protectively. 'It exists as it always has done and besides, Ethan isn't a writer he's an artist; he's a sculptor who sculpts narratives, not a novelist. He plays with collage and he is no more a plagiarist than Picasso was. Remember those lovely paintings inspired by the old masters? – he honours them and challenges us to look again; he used them for aesthetic reasons and Ethan uses Munro in a similar manner.

'Tuts,' Cathy replied, 'are ye thinkin' I came up the Clyde on a bike?' The twins stared at her. Only Finlay recognised her habit of retreating into vernacular when feeling threatened. 'I dinna mind a wee bit disagreement,' she continued, 'if it keeps the talk lang, but we have a sayin' hereabouts that a dram brings truth unco close and all it's done here is sent it scatterin'. But let's get on, I'm not one to moan for Scotland. The question is, are we making a book and if so are the two of you going to work together on the writing of it?' The men shared a look and a nod. Cathy turned to Ethan. 'I must warn you, Finlay's characters can be rather particular.' Ethan smiled. 'Then I think we should publish it. My mother has a friend who lives in Inverara. She must know someone in the Munro Society who we can approach with this. I'll ring her after supper and I'll inform James that his role has changed to that of publisher.' Her mobile chirped again. 'It's Andrew. He, James and Mary have just arrived. I will invite them to join us for supper.' Once she had completed her text message, Cathy gathered up her apron and returned to the kitchen.

The supper for seven was a great success and by the time the guests were leaving, Andrew had offered to add himself to the pool of writers. Not realising that the book was to be a surprise for Mairi, he told her about it on the phone and promised to include an account of her adventures to find a piper. Mary had agreed to write a foreword, providing that it also had a place in the novel, and James agreed to make a draft to present to the Munro Estate, before sending it to his printers for production.

Craig

When Craig swung a lover's arms round the bag of his pipes and his big drone filled the rafters, *the bothy roared with the tuning, and then the air came melting and sweet from the chanter. Eight steps up, four to the turn, and eight down went* Craig, *and the piobaireachd rolled to his fingers like a man's rhyming.* [19]

Mairi, Clyde and Duncan were astounded. *The March came fast to the chanter – the old tune, the fine tune that Kintail has heard before, when the wild men in their red tartan came over hill and moor; the tune with the river in it, the fast river and the courageous that kens not stop nor tarry, that runs round rock and over fall with a good humour, yet no mood for anything but the way before it. The tune of the heroes, the tune of the pinelands and the broad straths, the tune that the eagles of Loch Duich crack their beaks together when they hear, and the crows of that country-side would as soon listen to as the squeal of their babies.* [20]

'You have the tartan of the clan in it,' cried Duncan when the tune was finished.

'And how does the lass tak' it,' Craig asked.

'Beautiful and even better,' Mairi said, 'but there are march tunes and lyrical tunes and it's not usual that the marches carry the day. Would you not play for us something in the lyrical mode?'

Craig laughed. *He put his fingers on the holes, and his heart took a leap back over two generations, and yonder was Glencoe! The grey day crawled on the white hills and the black roofs smoked below. Snow choked the pass, eas and corrie filled with drift and flatted to the brae-face; the wind tossed quirky and cruel in the little bushes and among the smooring lintels and joists; the blood of old and young lappered on the hearthstones, and the bairn, with a knifed throat, had an icy lip on a frozen teat. Out of the place went the tramped path of the Campbell butchers – far on their way to Glenlyon and the towns of paper and ink and liars.*

At its end, Duncan uttered words like a prayer: '*Muinntir a' ghlinne so, muinntir a' ghlinne so! People, people, people of this glen, this glen, this glen!*'[20] Had there been a Diamaid or two nearby he'd have dirked them.

Clyde was standing by the door, white and rigid, too frightened even to take to his heels. Mairi sat with tears streaming down her cheeks, as did young Coll, but knowing that there was nothing for it but another dram, he picked up the bottle and offered it.

'*Slainte Mhath*, Good Health,' said Duncan, 'you're a piper with a story right enough. So Mairi, it's certain then that you'll not be having this tune for ye weddin'.

'I'm exhausted,' said Mairi, 'completely wrung out. I never heard the like of it.'

Clyde stepped forward, tripped over a stool, fell on the table and upended it, sending every object on it into the air. He landed next to the table, which was standing vertically, dazed and covered in cake and water. Luckily Coll still had the whisky in his hand. He asked Clyde if he was still in one piece and our hero laughed, rose to his feet and brushed himself down.

'Just adding a few battle effects,' he said and everyone joined him in the laughter.

'There'll be no more drinking for you my laddie, battle effects or no,' Craig told him.

Once they had returned the contents of the bothy to their rightful position, Mairi asked Craig what he would play if he were at a wedding.'

'Nothin',' was Craig's prompt and singular reply.

'Not even a special wedding, with friends, where the pay is good?' Mairi asked.

The old man raised his great eyebrows. 'I am not,' he said, *'a tinker's minstrel, to give my tuning for bawbees and a Quaich of ale. The king himself could not buy the tune I ken if he had but a whim for it.'* [20]

Mairi had no words to express her feelings, but she knew that she had insulted her fine host, so she went over to the old man, kissed him on the head and whispered the words, 'forgive me' to his ear. Craig took her hand, held it gently in his and smiled.

'I ken you know your music,' he said, 'and I'm sure you've good reason for wantin' fine entertainment, but I suspect you've been too long among the herded folk and now you're smirched with their ambitions of wantin' everythin' big and in an instant. You visit me and ask for a tune and it's yours without a fee, but you've got the wrong reckonin' if you imagine me travellin' abroad and sitting down at a weddin'. It'll never happen, no matter how much I love ye.'

'But will the traditions continue if you stay at home?'

'That's the ba' up on the slates noo,' Craig laughed. 'It's no the traditions that you're needin' at your weddin' is it? You're making it all up lass and you know't. Thar's plenty o' wonderful musicians in these isles, singers too, all o' 'em fine for any occasion whar music's needed. What's wrong wi' these folk? What is it that's getting' to ye about your weddin' that needs me? Is it the nerves?'

'No, I just wanted to chance on a piper. I didn't want to arrange him. I wanted to be lucky, for the sake of luck. You know, just as it was in the old way of doing things, not as herded folk do it.'

'Och, well if it's a chancy thing you're after then look at young Coll here. He's the lucky charm if ever there was one and he can play the pipes as well as any man.'

'Well enough to put new heart in my guests?'

'Aye, there's magic in him right enough and more to the point he looks the part. You've no seen 'im in 'is tartan, but I swar this laddie could put new heart in a granny. She'd even follow 'im up a mountain if that's whar he were headin'. That's magic for ye and he's more for weddin's than I am. Now make 'im an offer and I swar there'll be no hearts goin' home still wantin'.'

'It's not a difficult job,' she told Coll. 'the music just has to have a particular beauty to it.'

'Don't worry,' he said, 'I have the measure of beauty. I'll imagine mysel' on yon hill and put my heart in it.'

Mary

Mary's novels have statements on the back cover that give the impression that she is about to be nominated for a national book award; phrases like, 'No other writer can consistently produce surprise of this quality,' or, 'I applaud the subtlety, sharpness and depth of her observations.' These are statements that hold Finlay, Andrew and Ethan in awe of her and, knowing how clearly she would over-shadow them, they were most relieved when Mary showed no desire to enter their modest writing circle.

Andrew spent much of his time editing the text and with geometrical precision he ensured that each portrait took up an identical amount of space. James, having cleared the book's production with his printers, was assisting with the layout and they all agreed that, subject to obtaining consents from the Munro Estate, the book would be published on the wedding day. Cathy donated a water colour landscape for the front cover and she was now discussing the itroductory pages of the book with the Munro Estate.

They have all agreed that the book will be called Mairi's Wedding, believing that the ring of familiarity it gains from being associated with the popular song will be good for it. Andrew is to be the first name of the author, but it is to have Mairi's surname, which is Hendry, so that no known person can be credited with writing it.

On this day, Mary was considering the foreword. Her manner was full of mischief and, as she walked the room with her familiar limp, the disciplines of oration and eulogy were fixed firmly in her sights. She was in every sense a vision of concentration. With the conversation of the previous night's supper in mind, she addressed the empty room loudly, promenading confidently, and appealing to herself to give expression to the author's position with enough wit and eccentric wisdom to tell the truth of its very particular method of production.

'Should you be prepared,' she began, 'to judge this tale in a manner not in keeping with other novels, the act will undoubtedly prove itself worthy of the effort. The author of this work has chosen an unconscious starting point for no other reason than to ascertain the nature of his roaming. It is an important factor – why we choose to roam where we do – and while some may consider this a refusal to join in the accepted literary game, it is more correctly an attempt to find a new space to play in. If you imagine Hendry, purposefully darting round a library at full speed, chancing upon material and moving in close before he has time to doubt it, then this is the colourful tactic our author employs to distract his decision making and to locate himself in that kind of place where marvellous accidents can occur.'

Once she had the scent of her foreword, Mary opened her laptop to write these words and then she added a few more of a similar nature.

'If the narrative is to be believed, three of its characters are writing a series of portraits of the guests who are to attend Mairi's wedding. Each of the authors has a preoccupation. For Finlay it is character, for Andrew it's structure, and for Ethan it's the lyricism of Neil Munro's language. Pieces of Munro's text are used in this work almost as an artist uses components in a collage, an act that re-frames his literature and allows his beautiful prose to shine out.

'The poetic qualities of nineteenth century novels can be easily lost amidst the wealth of similar material that fills their pages, but this book is generous to Munro for it treats us to some of the best of him.

'There is an element of chance in the way that the borrowed texts and the original subjects have been selected and the attitude of casualness throughout seems to have a great significance for the work. At times whole paragraphs of Munro are quoted in full and at other times snippets of his texts or odd words are used without earning a reference. Sometimes the text elaborates upon or extends a theme and at other times its presence is used to create dissonance or surprise. Some quotes are given name or gender changes to ensure their alignment with the context, but other quotes are left intact despite the conflicts. In Christine's story a modern young Frenchman is described as wearing plaid and carrying a lantern and the invitation is that we should accept such a fashion.

'There are times when the tense of borrowed texts, a thing that is never changed, works against the language construction of the piece in which it is placed and this is a device that will either strain a reader's concentration or invite them to enjoy collision; a choice that is entirely the reader's.

'This is a collage of nineteenth century descriptions placed alongside events in the twenty-first century. It is a quilt of many different materials that work together in an opaque way and out of which the meaning, if there is one, rises up in the most gentle fashion. Speed, chance and play are crucial to it, for these are the elements that keep formality at bay. It is an author's exercise in acceptance, taking what he finds when he finds it and placing it in the collage before he has time to judge its importance.'

When she had finished, Mary showed it to Andrew and asked him for his opinion.

'Perfect,' he said, 'are you happy for it to be placed in the novel as it is?'

'Certainly,' Mary replied, 'just drop it in as you have dropped in everything else. I don't need any time to question it. Tell me one thing though...' and she stopped. She was not certain she should ask this, and then she decided she should. How does the novel end?'

'Well now... let me see,' Andrew began thoughtfully. 'The book arrives at the wedding while the guests are being entertained and so complete is their engagement that they do not notice it sitting quietly at a table. The book doesn't mind this in the least, because she is certain that it's her birthday they are celebrating, not a wedding and more importantly, she is so taken up with the conceit that she is going to become a major Hollywood movie that she hardly cares who reads her at the present time.'

Neil

Andrew received an email from his friend Neil.

'Andrew, I am worried that coming to your wedding will increase my unhappiness. The contrast between your happy situation and mine is too great. Last night I wrote to Sonya and the letter is attached. Do you think I should send it? Is it pathetic? Love, Neil.'

Here is the attachment.

Dear Sonya

I am trying my best to cure myself of my love for you. I have been seeing all kinds of women via the internet, most of them unsuitable, but I continue to date them. The Slovenian cultural theorist lectured me for the entire day on the social responsibilities of art and a Serbian psychotherapist (an existentialist and follower of Artaud) lectured me all night on the power of theatre. The managerial consultant, having recently fired a team of forty head hunters in the States, fired me on the first night and the consultant haematologist drew blood before finishing her first drink. The jolly painter did not believe in criticism, the writer never read poetry, the business psychologist wanted to be my agent, the archaeologist questioned my foundations and a film producer suggested that I should take a closer look at Walt Disney.

I do not wish to be rude to these women for the fault lies with me, with the obstinacy of my heart, with my inability to make new connections, but what can my poor heart do? You were like the promise of a rainbow. How could a heart not wish to love you? But enough of this. I know that I must banish the thoughts I once had of being a proud and independent man at your service and in silence suffer the consequences of creating for myself a fiction and an inappropriate dream.

You know something of this frail intelligence of mine that is so prone to self doubt, but could you not dwell longer on my compassion, that spirit in me that underlies my truth and gives expression to my art, for this is the place where we met? Like most people my gold lies mostly hidden, the memory of it only enlivened on rare occasions when fragments that have existed apart for thousands of years are somehow joined together and the dancing happiness floods in. With you, just when I least expected it, I had a glimpse of it, I had it in my hand, and now it is once again lost to me.

It is rare for someone to appear rainbow-like, out of nowhere, and act as a bridge to take another across territory that was formerly the place of their divided distractions. You connected my art to my passion; you joined the meaningless snippets of my life together and created singularity out of my fragmentary collage. We can rarely guess at a connection like this until it is directly upon us and even then we mostly take to the air in a glory of winged passion and then reject it all out of fear that it will not be possible to get back down again. You were like a window appearing from nowhere and giving sight of a scene I could never have imagined. You inspired me to gaze with eyes that have previously only informed my art, eyes that had never before shone with love. You were lovelier to me than gold and though your complexion never dimmed your summer season was all too short and now I am lost, wandering in the shade.

I loved the wonderful flights of generous attention you gave me and the inspiration I gained from your way with language and next to these fine attributes I had little to contribute but my failures. I tried desperately to be humorous and charming, but I suppose my old melancholy rose up again and quashed any chances there were for laughter. I would like to believe that my melancholy could be seen in a kinder light, for it is the nicest melancholy you could wish to find anywhere, bar that of one chap I know, but he is definitely too old and too far away to be a candidate for my replacement.

Could you believe that my melancholy doesn't run so deep? I know that being with me might feel like a cross country hike with an armadillo when you were expecting a walk in the park with the family pet, but lift the armour just a little and you will discover the sweetest fellow hiding there. I'm nervous, that's all, nervous and too much affected by the possibility of love. But I am never nervous for long and it's certain that I will not be so overwhelmed by your love after a year or so and then you will find that you have a very decent fellow at your side.

You might be the princess to my frog and discover that I am a prince. I wonder what caused the rupture before your kiss could be delivered to your kind and loyal frog? Maybe it was a case of too much too soon. A diet of abundant excitement was never high on a doctor's recommendations for curing melancholy. It can't have been the wildness, for this is an accomplished dance that we both share. What could have caused my banishment into cold waters where my rocky heart flounders? Why would someone as delightful and insightful as you throw away the key that opened my treasured chest? What could have turned our sweet hours into days of sour regret? How could I have made you feel that having my love was worth nothing more than you had before?

I adored the thought that my love was of some use to you and when I discovered that you undervalued it then the recession in me started and my anger arose. I am sorry for the horrid emails; I never believed you to be an unemotional robot. Can I make amends for my foolishness? Can I find a way of sharing my true feelings again? Surely there is something I can offer. Your understanding of the human spirit is without compare, so please look at me again. The hungry pain of my broken spirit is so acute that it's like a dagger through my heart.

If you can return to me, think of my words no more, be a rainbow again and give this frog a kiss on the head. You will never regret it. If you can't return to me, think of my words no more, be a rainbow, just once, and give this frog a kiss on the head so that he might believe that our love was real, even though its time was short.

My love always, Neil.

Andrew replied by text. 'Attend wedding, send letter.'

Annie

During a break between sets at the Jazz Cafe, Annie sent Mairi a text message. 'Booked flights. Must fly Saturday return Sunday. Tour going well, but schedule too tight. Love you.' Mairi's reply read, 'I've found a piper who can charm the birds. Can't wait to see you. Love Mairi.'

Mairi would have had Annie's band playing at the wedding but they were touring France. She loved Annie's bright voice, her fresh, clear tones, the intimacy and charm she brought to her love songs and she once told Annie that her singing connected affection with meaning.

'Well,' Annie replied, 'without the generous intimacy of my band I couldn't sing the truth of feelings. They can predict a change in tempo before I've taken a breath. They're the ones who find space for phrasing, I just occupy it with song.'

Mairi, wanting to convince Annie that she had the ability to send spirits soaring, pressed her point. 'Are you trying to tell me that in a *Piobaireachd* the piper's skilly tripling over the groundwork of the tune is nothing without a drummer's deep notes? It's the pipes that search out lyricism; it's the pipes that put an end to the whoop of the night hag and inspire bright memories of the ancient unperplexed days; it's the piper who helps folk to hear the carousing in the old shealings and its your singing, Annie that evokes the love we feel.'

Remembering this conversation, Annie smiled. She took a last searching glance at the audience and then joined her band for the second set. Being in France was a complex mixture of nervousness and exhilaration for Annie. She'd always had a yearning for the French and as a child she refused to eat her food unless her Mother first vouched for its genuine French pedigree. Chips had to be called French Fries and Pasta was Parisian Noodles.

Recently Annie had started to fantasize about marrying a Frenchman and since her arrival she had studied men with a very particular regard. This was the cause of her nervousness, but she was never nervous while singing - in this place she was in another world. She welcomed her audience back and introduced a song by Lionel Bart.

Where ere ere ere ere is love?
Does it fall from skies above?
Is it underneath the willow tree
That I've been dreaming of?
Where ere ere ere ere is he,
Who I close my eyes to see?
Will I ever know the sweet 'hello'
That's meant for only me?
Who can say where he may hide?
Must I travel far and wide?
'Til I am beside that someone who
I can mean something to,
Where ere ere ere ere,
Where ere ere ere ere is love?

Despite the rapture of her audience, there are few who could imagine how thoroughly Annie inhabits her songs. How each phrase lasts an age; how they start; the nature of their rising and falling; how they end – every element is crucial to how she feels, how she will feel when she remembers her successes with pleasure and her failures with pain. Annie is a sculptor of words; everything from their annunciation to their expression has meaning, even the quality of a 'd' at the end of 'hide' could have serious consequences for her well being. It's this ability to lose herself in a melisma, or the waver of a quaver that makes Annie an artist. Only an artist could inhabit so many layers of intention and reflection at the same moment.

Where ere ere ere ere is love?
Does it fall from skies above?
Is it underneath the willow tree
That I've been dreaming of?
Where ere ere ere ere is he,
Who I close my eyes to see?
Will I ever know the sweet 'hello'
That's meant for only me?
Every night I kneel and pray,
Let tomorrow be the day
When I see the face of someone who
I can mean something to,
Where ere ere ere ere,
Where ere ere ere ere is love?

The audience's clapping was ecstatic. Annie imagined them on a high plateau where they could see a great distance with intense clarity. Out of her many nuances within repetition she had created surprise for them and her continual interweaving of similar themes had acted upon them, transporting them to a territory, once familiar and now layered with meaning. Annie is pleased when she has captivated her guests without capturing them. To have breathed a little space into the smallest landscape and filled it with lyricism is, for her, love. She thanked her audience repeatedly and then informed them that the tempo was to change to a swing. The band started playing 'On a Misty Night,' a composition by Tadd Dameron, and Annie accompanied them with Georgie Fame's lyrics.

On a warm misty night like this,
I can't resist your charms.
Until dawn, darling I insist
That I exist in your arms.
Let the morning wait,
While we see-al our fate,
Love was born from a moment's bliss
With you on this misty night.

A person would have to be seriously hungry to take as much care over the delivery of a song as Annie does – that and the faith that it is possible, and grace; oh! so much grace must be in place to perform like this. And our good fortune is that we will never run short of singers who are willing to dedicate themselves to the task, who care enough to make simple things sparkle, who can unleash that part of themselves that has seen both joy and sorrow and, like ancient folk, will keep these songs in their hearts, travel with them to the far corners of the earth and give everything just to receive another song in return.

Eilidh

Wishing to make a good impression on the family who are soon to be Mairi's in-laws, Cathy arrived at the hotel early to plan how they might spend their first day. Mary introduced Cathy to her parents, William and Annabel, and to her Aunt Kirsty. The guests drank coffee and asked about who was who in Cathy's family without once touching upon their itinerary. Cathy, an enthusiastic speaker, described her grandparents, Alastair and Morag, her mother, Aileen and her deceased father, Ewan; she pictured for them her Aunt Janet, who died in France, leaving Emile, her husband, to bring up Sebastian and Christine and then she moved on to talk of her aunt, Eilidh, who was well known for her eccentricities.

'She's our queen of culture,' Cathy told them, 'and the art has kept her young. She bought a shop to sell books, music and paintings, but her poetry readings, musical events and art exhibitions are her real love and the reason for her acclaim.'

The guests, intrigued by Cathy's introduction, were quick to agree that a visit to Eilidh's 'cultural centre' would be the place they headed for first. During the car journey Cathy talked of Eilidh's daughter, Flora, who was born when her mother was an art student in Glasgow.

'Eilidh returned to the family,' Cathy told them, 'and she and Flora lived alone; she never told anyone who the father was. Flora is beautiful. She writes poetry, paints landscapes and sings in a band; not a Gaelic band you'll understand, but Eilidh is mighty keen on the Gaelic music and we could listen to some if you wish.'

The visitors entered the bookshop and Cathy called to her Aunt, who they found in the gallery, placing cards beneath the paintings being exhibited. Introductions were made and Eilidh invited them to the opening party.

'Tonight at six,' she informed them, 'and now you must tell me what you think of the paintings.'

Silence descended on the gallery.

'They are surprising,' Mary suggested thoughtfully, 'or maybe playful is the word I'm looking for. I don't really have enough experience to talk about them.'

Eilidh waited for other responses, but her guests were fixed in their serious gazes.

'Be brave,' she invited them. 'There's freedom here and their abstraction is deceptive. The territories that Lindsay imagines for his narratives tease into the sunlight what is generally left in the dark. They are gentle and modest and I think they invite smiles from the senses. I dislike art that grabs at you insistently and shakes you about.'

'They look like story-boards for a film,' Kirsty said, 'are they many pictures joined together?'

'Not really.' Eilidh smiled. 'Lindsay has a movie set for a mind though. His brush strokes are quick and they create unlikely moments of coincidence. For me, his use of black always invites the notion of shadows.'

'My word,' Kirsty exclaimed. 'I don't know how you can talk about them like that.'

'I like them,' William offered from a distance. 'I feel that I must continually switch the way I look at them and this gives me the feeling of going into them and out.'

'I look at them like that too,' Eilidh offered. 'I rehearse my connection to them. Sometimes I discover evidence that explains what's happening and sometimes I don't. They are never going to tell you everything; they like to wait quietly to be discovered.'

'Does he draw the scenes before he paints them? Annabel asked.

'No, he doesn't plan them; they arrive as he paints.'

'They do change,' Cathy added, staring at them intently with her eyes half closed. 'Sometimes I see figures, or faces and a bird. Look there's a bird, there.'

'It's the paint that invites it,' Eilidh laughed, 'that and the intimacy of the colours. Some people have said that they find them ominous, I don't know how, but maybe they are nervous about being in an unknown place that is not clearly depicted.'

'You're right about the story-board quality,' Annabel said. 'Sometimes though I think that the scenes, if there are any, have been painted over each other like a transparent collage. Maybe that's what people find ominous; they are familiar and yet they are not naturalistic.'

'No, but when we feel that there is only a slight shift away from the figurative, that's when we suspect that he has a scene in mind. He plays with tiny flickers of connection to create it.'

'Oh, you have to be dreaming with your eyes half closed to paint tiny flickers of connection,' Mary said.

'Quite right,' Eilidh responded, 'and good for him. There's not enough dreaming these days and without it we can't see the moon reflected in the water or a cave in the mountain side, and then we can't invite ourselves to go there and hide. Do you know what this reminds me of?' – she points to the canvas – 'a fellow leaning against a lamp post in a city where only children dream and play. And look at this. There's a blue sky in the east and stars in the west. I love dreaming like this; our memories need it, just as it enjoys a tune long after it's been heard.'

A loud clapping came from the doorway then and they all turned, startled.

'Lindsay,' Eilidh exclaimed, 'have you been standing there all this time?'

'Long enough to hear your eulogy,' Lindsay said.

Eilidh laughed and introduced her guests to the artist. Lindsay was expressive and charming with his greetings, but when Eilidh offered to make coffee he followed her to the kitchen. The guests gazed at them and watched as Lindsay placed his arm around Eilidh's shoulder, whispering soft words in her ear. They retreated to the bookshop then to browse the book shelves. The women took quick glances in the direction of the couple. Each imagined that Lindsay might be Eilidh's long lost lover, but none showed the slightest hint of their imagining. Later, when they were on the car journey to the harbour for lunch, William broke their uncharacteristic silence.

'Could Lindsay be the absent father of Flora?' he asked.

Sebastian

Sebastian, a drummer of some repute with a fine reputation for reckless living, had recently taken to self-reflection and had come to the conclusion that of late he had missed too many chances. What he did not realise was that he had missed even more opportunities than those he knew of, for there were many instances when he was in the wrong place at the right time and these occasions may well have changed his fate; the night when Annie was singing at the Jazz Café was one such instance.

Initially our young drummer let it be known that he was only going to the Highlands to please his father, but in truth his enthusiasm was instigated by an intriguing premonition. In this presentiment he was travelling to Scotland by boat and it took some considerable persuasion on his father's part before Sebastian agreed to forgo this idea and accompany him and Christine on the plane.

Once they had booked into their Scottish hotel, a place that was still a castle, his father phoned his sister-in-law, Aileen, who had arranged for the whole family to come there and welcome them. In the hotel lounge that evening there were a great number of conversations to be had, but it was Clyde, the hero of invented fantasies, who attracted Sebastian's attention most positively. Clyde, with a few spectacular additions of his own, related tales of his recent adventures with Mairi; their search for a piper to play at the wedding; how they had come across young Col and how Black Duncan this very day was transporting the piper here in his boat. Sebastian, much taken with these tales of the sea, expressed a desire to see the landscape by boat and after a short conversation with the hotelier, Clyde returned with the news that he had found a captain who was willing to take them on a tour of the islands.

On the following morning Clyde and Sebastian were standing together aboard the ancient vessel. *There was something in that chill grey monotone of sky and sea that filled* Sebastian *with a very passion of melancholy. The wind had risen, and the billows ran frothing from the east; enormous clouds hung over the land behind them, so that it seemed to roll with smoke from the eternal fires. The ship went fast, blown upon the frothy billows, like a ponderous bird, leaving a wake of hissing bubbling brine, flying, as it seemed, to a world that stretched infinitely into a region very grey and chill. Oh, the pallor! Oh, the cold and heartless spirit of the sea in that first dawning morn!* [21]

It seemed no time at all before our new friends observed panic among their trusted crewmen and then they heard the captain roar that the anchor must be dropped. *She might be Charon's craft pausing midway on the cursed stream, and waiting for the ferry cry upon the shore of Time. They were still in the estuary or firth, to judge by the bickering burn and the odours off-shore, above all the odour of rotting brake; and they rode at anchor, for her bows were up-water to the wind and tide, and above them, in the darkness, they could hear the idle sails faintly flapping in the breeze and reef-points all tap-tapping.* [22]

Sebastian stared at *the enormous ocean, cruel, cold, spread out to the line of the streaming halliards and clew-garnets, the spray buffeting upon their hull and spitting in their faces like an enemy.* He could *hear the tumult of the seamen hurrying vulgarly to save their wretched lives, the gluck of waters in the bowels of the ship, the thud of cargo loose and drifting under decks.* [23]

Everyone manned the life-boat, Clyde keeping up a constant monologue with himself, Sebastian berating the bad luck that had been dogging him for months. The small craft was thrown upon the foreshore and once they had scrambled across the dunes, relief began to make itself felt. Our two adventurers stayed with the sailors, accompanying them over the hills on their journey home. Upon reaching a hamlet they *came across a hostel that sent out a most hearty reek and firelight, the odours of stewing meats and of strong waters, and the sound of piping and trumping and laughing.* [24] It was the very answer to their prayers.

The landlord served them a jug of ale and listened to the Captain's sorry tale. Sebastian, enthralled by the merriment of the house, drummed with his hands on the table as though charm itself issued from the tunes that zigged from the fiddler.

A bold tall man with very black eyes and lambent eyes, hiccoughing with drink but not by any means drunken, came up to him.

'Would you like your fortune spaed sir?' asked my *black friend, twitching his thumb in the direction of his wife, who was leering back with a friendliness begot of the bottle. The place was full of deafening noises and peat smoke* and Sebastian told the man that from past experiences with fortune tellers this was not a thing he was keen to repeat. *'Still and on,'* said he, *'who knows but you may find a wife and a good fortune in a little lurk of the thumb? Jean! Jean! woman,'* he cried across the chamber to his callet, and she came to a very indifferent and dubious client.[25]

'There's a young woman, a singer by all accounts, who's waiting for ye,' the woman said, scrutinising Sebastian's hand and looking surprised by what she found.

'That's not reading the hand at all,' Sebastian replied. 'Such small facts of life are never written in a line on a hand. You are making the whole thing up.'

'She can find life's history in the space of a hair,' her husband whispered. 'Do not disturb her now.'

'She's hereby,' the good woman insisted, 'but be quick to capture her before another takes her fancy,' and with that she left Sebastian's company to her husband.

The black-eyed fellow told Sebastian that before paying the fee he should know his information, for it would leave him more satisfied than his wife's reading had done. For this the young drummer was asked to pay double. Sebastian, bemused, paid up and the fellow told him that his wife was at his hotel last evening and had overheard Mairi chatting with a friend of hers, called Annie, and she, while performing in France, was looking for a husband.

Flora

The first time Flora saw Mr. Webster he was standing on a ladder in her back garden collecting fish off the rose bushes. The evening was warm, its red spread out against the sky, and young Flora stood gazing at the man for some time before asking him how he came to be there. He told her that he was the new tenant, living in the flat above the gallery, but he did not stop his fish gathering to tell her this, nothing could distract him from his single minded ambition to retrieve the fish. Being cooked, the fish broke into pieces as he stretched to gather it. He had a pan in one hand and a fish slice in the other and Flora imagined that he was probably a knight of ancient Gaeldom who had returned to perform some sacred rite.

Not content with capturing those pieces of fish that had departed from the whole, Mr. Webster began stretching his long limbs far into the bush to retrieve the main skeleton. His fish slice flashing in the sunlight, he sought to release those exposed bones that had become entwined with the branches and those gluttonous pieces of fish that stuck to the bones. Undeterred, and oblivious to the danger, Mr. Webster then began to flick with his fish slice and, regardless of the size of flesh that flew into the air, he stretched out his pan to catch what he could. After each twist and turn, the ladder slipped further into the bush and Mr. Webster let out great cries of pain as the thorns grazed his skin.

Later, when he was explaining how the fish came to be there, great tears of laughter were rolling down his cheeks. The rose bushes were directly beneath his kitchen and the fish had slipped from his frying pan out of the window as he was moving the pan to the sill to make room on his two-ring hob for a pot of peas. Flora had never before seen a man laugh so heartily and neither had she seen laughter accompanied by tears. She wondered then if it was a common thing for these two actions to occur at the same time, but she never got round to asking Mr. Webster if this was so.

Flora's summer months with Mr. Webster were the happiest of her life. Being an only child, living miles from any children who were of interest to her, Flora had become accustomed to games with only her voice to narrate them, but in Mr. Webster's company she grew to love his chatter and the stories he told. He was a comic and completely at ease with her, but most importantly for Flora he never hid his vulnerability, just as she never hid hers. Later, on those rare occasions when she was with men, she studied them carefully to determine if they too might possess Mr. Webster's kind of comic vulnerability, but none appeared to do so.

When Flora listened to her school friends talk about boyfriends, she could never be certain of her feelings and when she suspected that a fellow might be attracted to her it was only nerves that she experienced. One day, instead of taking the bus straight home, she stayed in town with her friends and a boy, taking her by the arm, told her that he knew she would be there to meet him. Flora asked how he could know such a thing and he told her that it was because he wished it. Flora eyed him suspiciously and could not understand the connection he spoke of.

'It is something that lies between men and women,' he told her, 'and it always happens when they are really fond of each other.'

Flora found the boy's talk attractive and when they parted she allowed him to kiss her, but she cried on the bus. At home she threw her arms about her mother's shoulders and placed her head on her breast, just as she had done as a child. Reading the signs of her daughter's distress, Eilidh did not question her lateness, but invited her to speak of those things that had upset her.

'Oh mother it's beyond me,' Flora replied. 'I just want to laugh and cry at the same time. I'm that happy it makes me dizzy and so miserable it gives me the frights.'

'Ar't a little dipped in love my lass?' Eilidh asked, and Flora nodded and bit her lip. 'But you're just a slip of a lass and you'll soon learn that these feelings are not enduring.' After these words they fell silent and Eilidh hugged the child and fell to thinking what she might say to ease the malady. Thoughts came to her right enough, but she could not put them into words. That love is a honey-sweet thing that must sometimes be salted with our tears was a sentiment too difficult for Flora to comprehend. Some Gaelic words came to Eilidh then and she uttered them softly. 'Love is the age of gold and there is not a pleasure under heaven that is finer than the pain of it.' Flora nodded and wiped her tears, comforted by the Gaelic without understanding a word of it.

'I wish that I could be a child again,' Flora said. 'I would love to be in the garden laughing with Mr. Webster. With him the flowers were full of life and the world was at its best. When he told me stories about listening to the song of the blackbird and hearing the music of the stars, the birds and stars were like members of my family.'

This nostalgia remained with Flora for sometime and just as its power was beginning to wane another man came into Flora's life and brought it back again. This new man told Flora that he wanted to protect her, but Flora knew that he wanted to possess her. She felt ravished by the delirium in his eyes; by the way he languished in her soft, silken neck and it made her ill to think of it. She wrote to him, instructing him not to visit her again, but last night she dreamt that she was walking along a path between a slow moving canal and a fast flowing river that sped in the opposite direction. Flora did not know what to do, whether or not to move and if she did move which direction to take. The terror of indecision woke her and made that morning's breakfast a shaky affair.

Towards lunchtime, just as she was ironing the dress she would wear for Mairi's wedding, she thought again of Mr. Webster and the memory of his antics brought a smile to her face. 'A jolly adventure, that is what's needed,' she told herself firmly and there and then she ceased her ironing, went down the lane, caught the bus to the city and shopped until she had a bright new dress to wear.

Emile

Emile was eager to visit his sister-in-law alone, but he could not refuse his daughter, Christine, who wanted to accompany him. On their arrival, Emile made the happy discovery that Cordelia, Aileen's granddaughter, was also visiting there and he asked the young girl if she would give Christine some instruction in the Scottish customs. By the time Emile and Aileen had finished drinking their tea they had rediscovered a little of the affinity they had enjoyed in earlier years.

'Your children appear to be in fine form,' Aileen told him. 'Was it not a difficult thing to explain things to them when Janet died?'

'Oui,' Emile replied, 'I was err... careful, you know, not to be the adult who was responsible to explain how everything happens. I never wanted to upset their... um... how do you call it... their enchantment, non? Things function even when we don't know why they do, I think. Just like fairytales eh? They delight experience and engage enchantment without asking for understanding. These things are objects d'art, non? How we come to them ca c'est trés important. La particularité de la littérature ca c'est trés important.' Then he returned to the English. 'It's the same with the difficult things in life, I think.'

'My, but you're full of the enchantment right enough.'

'Of course, it's good for you, just as this landscape is. Cependant, I do not like this castle we stay in, it's haunted, j'en suis certain.'

'Every place here is haunted,' Aileen laughed.

'I bought this in Eilidh's bookshop,' he then said, holding up a book. 'The Gaul in the land of the Gael.' There are a good many fairies in here. In one of the stories a French Lieutenant falls in love with a local girl and while he is combing her yellow hair he discovers that it is made of sand. Then, because she is discovered she has no alternative but to take up her own form and return once again to the sea.'

'Well you can test my locks if you wish,' Aileen told him, holding up a lock of her hair. Emile gazed at it, not certain whether he should touch it or not.

'I know you well enough, Aileen,' he said. 'A fairy you might be, but you are a mortal one I think.' Emile took out the book and flicked the pages. 'There is a lovely tale in here about a young girl who yearns to meet a Sea-Fairy and she sits on the shore singing to them. Ah, here it is; this is her song. *Little folk, little folk, come to me, from the lobbies that lie below the sea.* And before she has finished singing a male fairy stands before her. She does not understand his fairy speech, but she understands her feelings for him. It is very beautiful. Please, the language is very nice; would you read some to me?'

Aileen smiled and taking up the book she began to read from that place in the story where Emile indicated with his finger.

And that way their friendship began.

At the mouth of many nights when the fishing-boats were off at the fishing, or sometimes even by day when the father and her two brothers were chasing the signs of sea-pig and scart far down on Tarbert, Marseli would meet her fairy friend in a cunning place at the Blackwater-foot, where the sea puts its arms well around a dainty waist of lost land. Here one can see Loch Finne from Ardno to Strathlachan: in front lift the long lazy Cowal hills, and behind is Auchnabreac wood full of deer and birds. Nowadays there is a road round about this cunning fine place, but then it lay forgotten among whins that never wanted bloom, and thick, soft, salty grass. Two plantings of tall trees kept the wind off and the centre of it beaked in warm suns. It was like a garden standing out upon the sea, cut off from the throng road at all tides by a cluster of salt pools and an elbow of the Duglas Water.

Here the Sea-Fairy was always waiting for the girl, walking up and down in one or other of the tree-clumps. He had doffed his fine clothes after their first meeting for plain ones, and came douce and soberly, but aye with a small sword on his thigh.

The girl knew the folly of it; but tomorrow was always to be the last of it, and every day bought new wonders to her. He fetched her rings once, of cunning make, studded with stones that tickled the eye in a way the cairngorm and the Cromalt could never come up to. [26]

Aileen read it to the end and discovered that the Sea-Fairy was actually a French wine trader and when it was discovered that he had been watering down the wine, he was keen to return to France before his purchasers could punish him.

Aileen was laughing about the poor reputation of the Frenchman when Christine and Cordelia returned.

Christine informed her father that Cordelia had taught her some Gaelic songs and he asked for a recital, but his daughter declined. Aileen then asked her granddaughter to sing for them, but she too was reluctant. When Aileen pressed her further, Cordelia's only compromise was to perform a dance. They agreed to this and Cordelia busied herself with moving the furniture around. After lighting candles she closed the curtains.

Then, slowly, our young heroine *plucked up the edges of her skirt in outstretched hands and started humming softly to herself an appropriate tune. The candles warmly lit her neck, her ears and her tilted nostrils; her brow was high in shadow. First she rose on tiptoe and made her feet to twitter on the flags, then swayed and swung a little body that seemed to hang in the air. The white silk swept around and over her – wings with no noise of flapping feather, or swirled in sea-shell coils, that rose in a ripple from her ankles and swelled in wide circling waves above her head, revealing her in glimpses like some creature born of foam on fairy beaches, and holding the command of tempest winds.* Emile *watched, entranced.* Cordelia *was a passion disembodied, an aspiration realised, a happy morning thought, a vapour and a perfume of flowers. She was the spirit of spring; he knew that he had felt it long ago in little woods, or seen it in pictures, or heard it in songs; she was an ecstasy, she was a dream.*[27]

Alban

It was in Birmingham, Alabama, that a group of young black lads discovered the look of wearing their breeks without a belt so that the waist of 'em would slip down below their bottoms. In the local State Penitentiary prisoners were often given trews that were too big for 'em and as belts were not provided they took to shuffling around, beyond caring about the drop of their garments.

This was the look that the laddies on the street wanted, for they associated more with the poor fellows in the Pen than they did with the 'respectable' inhabitants of their city. 'It looks so stupid. How on earth do their trousers stay up? It must be so uncomfortable.' These were the cries on everyone's lips and it pleased the street lads enormously to hear their comments.

'Yeah,' they said to themselves, 'how we keep going is a complete mystery to you, because you don't even know who we are.'

So this is how 'low-waist walking' started and it fulfilled beautifully the need in boys to have a way to express confidence in their vulnerability.

When others in other places saw how annoyed the 'respectable' people were getting over this gawkit fashion, they also took to the performance of it and before long the hooded boys in all the major cities of the States had started wearing their breeks in this low fashion and trauchled along lazily. By the time the craze hit the Lowlands, and the white guys were also at it, there was nothing to be done about it. Everyone was surprised that they too needed to express disaffection and disenchantment, but everyone accepted that the expectation that boys would dress presentably was a hopeless ambition.

At the time of this story, it was the Teacher's young son, Alban, who was enjoying the possibilities that this fashion provided. Alban's mother could ask him to pull his trews up countless times in day, and Alban would do so, knowing that in minutes they would be down about his thighs again. Mairi's wedding, however, was not a day that Alban was going to be victorious in dress, because he, like it or not, had already lost the costume argument.

'Ye'll nae gather with fantoosh guests like a disreputable rascal, I can tell ye that for sure,' his mother had told him when they were arguing about it. 'There maybe times when you can look like an unco scoundrel or a sculduddery loon, but a weddin's nae the time for it, so you'd best make sure that the kilt looks respectable.'

'I'm not wearing a kilt,' Alban insisted.

'Well ye'll nae go ootby dressed in trews on that day m'laddie I can tell ye that. Ye'll be wearing the feileadh or ye'll go naked, so you can make ye choice.'

So a kilt it was and today it was laid out on his bed with his jacket, shirt and tie. Alban considered his chances of leaving the belt at home. He pulled off his jeans and tried on the kilt. He was no more than a rickle o' banes, but the kilt without a belt would not fall far enough to make any kind of statement. The side straps were going to keep it up, come what may, unless – and he was thinking very hard on this point – unless the strap broke. Suddenly Alban saw the light and, picking up his Sgian Dubh, the short ceremonial dagger that he would wear in his stocking, he began scoring it into one of the straps. 'Just enough to cause it to snap after a little wear,' he told himself.

Alban's mother and sister, Heather, greatly distracted with their own attire, did not bother to check on the activities of young Alban. He listened to their excited chatter as he sat in a dwam, deepening the incision his blunt dirk made in the leather.

'Enough of your flichterie blethering,' his mother declared to her daughter after some time of the chatter, 'we must get on wi' our business or we'll ne'er be ready.'

'Oh, please,' Heather pleaded, 'Tell me more yet. Tell me in the Hielan' tongue how two people agree to get married.'

'Och now,' her mother replied, 'it's nae so hard. The would-be hain gives his would-be wifie a smuirch and if it don't glif her when he's beukin', he can go to his speerin'.

Heather understood everything and nothing of the meaning of her mother's little speech and the not understanding gave her considerable merriment.

'What's speerin'?' she asked.

'It's askin' the father for his daughter's hand in marriage,' her mother replied.

'Then I prefer the not knowing,' Heather told her

mother and the pair of them fell about laughing without declaring the exact cause of it.

Meanwhile Alban had finished his wilful task with the dirk. He kept well out of sight for the remainder of the morning and assumed a sweet and friendly air whenever his mother was nearby. Now and then she shouted, 'are ye set for off, laddie,' and once she asked why he was 'scutterin' aboot,' but she did not check on his progress.

By the time they were supposed to begin their walk to the Kirk, Alban, who was waiting outside for his father to arrive, was holding his arm close to his waist to prevent his kilt from dropping to the ground. The strap holding his kilt had already snapped and he was in a bit of a guddle about it. As neither his mother nor his sister had yet appeared, he decided that there was still time for restorative action. He ran ramstam up the stairs to his bedroom and began looking for his galluses to keep the kilt up, but he could not find them.

'I ken hear ye pechin' bairn,' his mother cried. 'Is there somethin' you're scutterin' aboot fir? I dinna want ye runklin' you're costume now.'

'Don't girn, mother,' Alban replied, and the fly laddie, finding a piece of string in his bed, tied it about him and, buttoning his jacket, presented himself ready for the ceremony. Once outside, his father, not used to seeing his son so tidy, ruffled Alban's hair. His mother, tutting loudly, licked her fingers and made it neat again. Heather smiled mockingly at her brother, but Alban did not react, he knew well enough that they would see another side of him before this day was out.

Part 2
The Wedding

Intrigue and Sabotage

Poor Alban, there's naught for a boy of nine to be doing at a wedding. He fiddled about during the ceremony, earning a clip or two from his mother, and pushed his food about his plate during the meal. Now and then Black Duncan caught his eye and sent him a wink of encouragement and as soon as the boy was allowed to leave the table he went over to the old mariner to make his acquaintance.

Knowing the power that a few tales of danger might have over a young lad, Duncan soon charmed the pants off young Alban and when he had every bit of the boy's attention, Duncan asked him if he was up to helping an old sailor carry out a task that was full of danger.

'Sure,' Alban replied, as though such an enterprise was nought but a typical day's work for a lad like him, and he sat in close to the old mariner as he related his tale.

'I'm goin' to tell ye of young Coll,' he began, 'the piper who's to play at the weddin'. Now this young laddie 'as been raised as a piper on moor and headland and, while the great ootdoors enjoys his airy talents, the more I heard him at close quarters the more I was certain that there was not enough romance in 'is piping fir a weddin'. D'ye ken? It was not goin' to suit the folk hereaboots and it were certainly not up to the mark for the very particular task that Mairi has in mind for 'im.'

'Does she want something to set her guests dancing?' Alban asked.

'No lad, more, much more and if I'd the time I'd tell ye the poetry of it. So now, after worryin' the issue over for many a night, I came to the conclusion that I had no alternative but to follow my sense of it; I had to teach my piper how to accompany Gaelic songs on the wee pipes. During the time of our sailin' here I had young Coll with me for a good few days and after lecturin' him on the need for musicians to share their knowledge, I started in to sing him the finest old songs I know.

'He was quick to pick up the accompaniment on the wee pipes, I'll give him that, but I knew that there was too much pride in him to accept this role for the weddin'. I had no way of persuadin' him politely to give another the spot light he was seekin', d'ya ken? so the use of guile is my only option and I need your help for it.'

Alban nodded his head confidently, giving the impression that he had been raised on intrigue and there was nothing he did better than sabotage.

'As soon as I was on dry land I introduced Coll to Cordelia,' the mariner continued, 'and it wasna long before their attraction was magic. I arranged for 'em to spend many an hour in each other's company and together we sang the ancient songs. Cordelia had learned them from me before this time so it wasna long before the two of 'em were settin' the heavens alight with their music. Och, I canna tell ye how excitin' it is to hear 'em.

'Does Cordelia sing with the romance you're after?' Alban asked.

'Indeed she does lad, there's none finer than Cordelia at the singing. So and on, and now I'm coming to the real bit of it. What we have to achieve is the wreckin' of the boy's bagpipes and we have to do it but moments before he is about to play, for if Coll discovers his bag ruined any time in advance some good samaritan is bound to run off and find him a replacement set. There also has to be shock in it, dae ye ken? I need to jump up and save the day with my suggestion that Cordelia could do the singing and tell them that Coll had already learned to accompany her on the wee pipes. As I see it, that's our only hand.'

Alban, his face alight with excitement, remembered in an instant every sequence of adventure he had stored in his memory. 'How do we wreck his pipes?' he asked.

'You have to do it boy. You have to spear his bag with ye dagger and no one must catch sight of ye doin' it.'

A Sudden Connection

Duncan instructed Alban to stick close to the piper right up to the moment he was about to play and then he introduced the boy to Coll and Cordelia. They were busy at their music in the garden. Duncan asked Cordelia to discover from her Aunt Mairi when she expected the music to begin and he asked Coll if he would show Alban the wonders of his bagpipes. Our young renegade kept the piper busy with his questions and his charming of Coll with compliments was carried out in such excellent fashion that Duncan had every reason to feel proud of his accomplice.

Cordelia returned before long with her Aunt's reply – The entertainment would start soon enough and the girl was not to bother her Aunt further with her excited and impatient demands, for she must judge the timing of its beginning most carefully. With this Duncan confirmed his sense that timing would be the most difficult aspect of this mission.

Alban, with nothing in the way of jitters for the task ahead of him, sat in sublime contentment listening to the sounds that Coll and Cordelia created. All he could think was that Duncan was his hero and he would do anything to please him. A sudden deepening connection was also the way of it for Donald and Murdo. They were out taking the air, but when they passed by and the singing was upon them they felt compelled to stop and listen. It is certain that as soon as the song was at an end and their stunned silence was no more, the friendship between them could not have been closer had they been siblings. In no time at all they had agreed that Donald was to take up permanent residence with Murdo at Castle Quair.

Then a van pulled up the driveway and Donald and Murdo went up to meet it. The driver handed them a cardboard box with Cathy Mackenzie's name on it and the happy pair went off to deliver it to her.

'It's the books,' Cathy mouthed to her husband and opening the box she took out a copy and thumbed its pages. Handing it to Finlay with the words, 'it looks splendid,' she awaited his verdict. It was a while in coming and when it did it was *'Slochd-a-chubair gu bragh!'* – the rallying cry of the Inneraora burghers.

'What?' Cathy asked, surprised, 'is that good or is there a mistake with the printing?'

'Och, its perfect, right enough,' her husband replied, 'but there's stuff in the book that has yet to happen in life, so we must give them their present later,' and with that he returned the book to its box and hid it under the table.

The heroic quartet, singer, piper, mariner and saboteur, then entered the hall and Coll indicated to Mairi that he was ready to begin. Alban was close behind him with the fateful dagger hidden up his sleeve. Mairi judging the moment auspicious, raised herself, clapped her hands and asked everyone to gather facing the stage where Coll was about to play for them.

Alban's mother motioned for her son to join her, but Alban hid behind Coll, pretending he hadn't noticed her bidding. Cordelia sat with her parents; Duncan stood to the side and as Coll made for the stage, Alban flicked the piper's heel with his foot and Coll fell sprawling upon the steps. The young lad bent to assist him and dropping the dagger from sleeve to hand he quickly pierced the piper's bag. All proceeded as planned. Coll tried to fill his bag, he discovered that it would hold no air and after examining it, found a hole. He showed this to a distraught Mairi and soon the state in the hall changed from festive merriment to horrified disarray. Duncan leaped forward.

'Dear guests, there's a solution,' he cried. 'Young Coll here is well accomplished on the wee pipes too and if Cordelia would join him in singing, the pair will make as fine an entertainment as ever you heard hereabouts.'

The First Day of Spring

Nervousness at the start of a performance is common enough, but you would have to multiply the worst condition known to you many times over to come close to imagining the kind of tension that filled the hall when Cordelia and Coll stood silently facing their audience. If you add to this the collective feeling of shock that still prevailed, this was the condition that continued unabated until the sound of Coll's pipe broke the anxious stillness.

Cordelia looked pale and her audience felt the passing of every second as they gazed at the rapid heaving of her bosom during Coll's introduction. As the first shaky tremors from her vocal chords issued forth, they were close to collapse, but then, like a bird taking flight, the young girl's voice suddenly matured and all were transfixed by the wondrous sound that came to them as sweet as a silver bell. With each song Cordelia became more confident; she charged every new phrase with deeper feeling and she brought new meaning and delight to the time-worn words of Gaeldom that she was honouring with her singing.

The look on Duncan's face was beatific. He was travelling through space, past the transient stars to a place where he was Lord of the Universe. New winds sighed from the mountains and cleared the old mists that had been mustering in the glens. Water that had long stagnated in hidden burns and secret wells flowed again, washing the land and filling the air with fresh scent as it soaked the wrack on pebbled beaches. The sea became calm, as clear as a mirror, and the birds, perching in the trees, piped at a golden sunset that flamed across the western sky. The old mariner had returned to an ancient empire where poetry was on the lips of all and the folly of love was behind every action.

Cathy, amazed by her daughter's powerful presence, slipped into a swoon. For her, the sound of the pipes came in from the sea, from a great expanse of bright blue ocean. She too could smell perfume on the air, but her fragrance was a rich scent that issued from the garland of red roses that Cordelia wore on her head. She saw herself in a sunlit garden, bathing in the beauty of its green, and her daughter, now grown miraculously tall, was in possession of a voice that had the magic to reverberate across mountains and echo through every glen.

After six songs the young singer fell silent and gave her mentor a questioning look. Duncan smiled broadly and nodded his head. Cordelia, uncertain what to do next, lifted her shoulders just a little and told the assembled guests that her recital must now be at an end for she knew no more songs to sing them.

With the sudden sound of applause, Cathy rose up from her dream and realised that everyone was as taken by her daughter's singing as she was. Just as the first day of spring surprises, so they were surprised by the brightness and warmth that filled the hall. Love sprung into the air and everyone felt young and excited at the prospect of starting anew. All was joyful relief and suddenly the guests were discovering new connections between them; the heat of it spurring some to remove garments. Many held hands, some kissed and smiles of blessing were everwhere, all of them little offerings that spoke of love.

Cordelia ran to her parents and the happy family hugged and kissed. Finlay sat his daughter upon his knee and Cordelia asked if he had enjoyed her singing.

'Enjoyed it, mercy me, but there's no words for it. It was sweet enough to change the very natures of us all. There's genius in you, my young lass.'

'Oh, I'm not sure that I was thinking of genius,' the young girl replied, 'it was gorgeous entertainment that I was after.'

'Well, you have that and something better, my lass, you have love to offer and there's nothing finer.'

As the Moon throws the Clouds apart

While Mary had been watching and listening to Cordelia her feet had beat time with the music and her face, flushed with heavenly transport, had displayed a smile, so sweet, so beautiful and so sensible to the glory of those moments that any soul who happened by chance to gaze in her direction would have felt compelled to dream in all its loveliness.

It was Ethan's eye that briefly gazed in Mary's direction and at that moment he secretly wafted a vagabond kiss off his fingertips in her direction. Mary, conscious of this act, *tossed her hair from her temples as the moon throws the cloud apart and beamed brightly and merrily and sent him back his symbol with a daring charm.*[28]

Neither turned a second time to engage the tender encounter, but the taste of it lingered all the while that Cordelia captivated their hearts and just as her magical refrains made apparent the possibility of sweet communication, so their lips displayed a smile of the wonder and pleasure of their new connection.

As soon as the tumultuous applause died away, Ethan and Mary walked towards each other as though everything they had read or written had been preparing them for this moment. It was the timeless message of bird and flower, of wave and wind, that they heard and, after feeding on the high, constant notes of Cordelia's singing, they bathed in the certain knowledge that this was indeed how the world had always filled its heart.

They placed their arms about each other and Ethan asked Mary to tell him the date of her birth. He asked it as though it were the most natural question in the world, but when Mary replied 'The 25th January,' Ethan let out a surprised exclamation.

'It's the date of Rabbie Burns's birth and death, he told her and as Ethan took Mary's hand in his, electricity flowed between them of the most beneficent kind and their eyes deliciously drew each other in.

'Have you read Burns's letters to Clarinda?' Ethan asked. Mary shook her head; she did it slowly so as not to lose the contact that flowed between them and, as she brought her free hand up to touch his cheek, she asked him to tell her about the letters.

'I haven't read them,' Ethan told her, 'but I should like to. Neil Munro mentioned them in a story called, 'Burns and Clarinda' and it concerned the poet's first letter to a woman he had recently met. Munro tells us that Burns thought Clarinda such a gloriously amiable and fine woman that he felt bound to declare his love for her, for the usual expressions of esteem and respect common to letters was altogether too tame to contain his feelings.'

The couple stood in silence 'til Mary asked Ethan if he remembered the words that Burns wrote to Clarinda.

Ethan was certain that he did not, but suddenly they came to him as though they had been carried by the air and it gave him some great surprise.

Oh Clarinda! Shall we not meet in a state, some yet unknown state of being where the lavish hand of plenty shall minister to the highest wish of benevolence, and where the chill north wind of prudence shall never blow over the flowery fields of enjoyment! If we do not, man is made in vain. [29]

'I'll not let you live in vain,' Mary told him and they kissed and it was like a wave washing the beach, a wave that gently bathed the euphoria that was the essence of their new intimacy.

'I don't mind how we meet,' Ethan declared, 'my only wish is that we should continue to meet all our days.'

'Good,' Mary chimed with delighted satisfaction and before kissing him slowly and purposefully on the lips she whispered, 'may we live forever.'

A Voyage of Ecstasy

Christine gazed at Neil's beautiful neck, at the strength of his chest that opened out beneath his shoulders; shoulders that seemed to promise her protection and embrace. Neil's body spoke to her; it filled her with yearning, not passion so much as a great calm that she associated with arriving home.

Many times in her short life Christine had the hint of a conviction that the bliss of deep attraction might one day be hers, but it was a delicate expectation, fairy-like and insubstantial. Now, she imagined herself clasping hold of this intangible thing; she had the sight of its form before her, she could embrace it, and she offered her submission to these sensations and the magnetism that flowed from this young man.

No words came to her, but Christine could hear the blood coursing through her body and she shivered at the thought that a new world was dawning, that she was about to embark on a voyage of ecstasy and arrive at the place where she truly belonged.

Neil was looking out to the far distance, his thoughts utterly content as he half closed his eyes on the incoming waves. He was imagining a boat out there that was his.

'At last it's coming in,' he whispered to himself, and then he turned and saw Christine, her lips, full of promise, frozen, about to speak. Her eyes, great shining orbs, were fixed on him and her breath, in deep sighs, was visibly moving her breast. In that instant Neil hoped that the reason for her visible delight might be something akin to the feelings he was experiencing.

'Could it be that our feelings are shared?' he asked, and immediately their hands joined together and their yearning was placed soundly into each other's keeping. They felt a continuity with all that was simple and ancient and they were unconscious of everything around them.

It was the barely audible gulp of surprise that came from Neil, mid kiss, that caused Christine to come out of her daydreaming and, while her own glazed eyes had not their usual focus, she looked into his and saw tears.

'Is it us or the music do you think?' Neil asked.

'Both,' was Christine's whispered reply.

'I am now so sensitively charged that I cannot think what to do first and I fear that without doing something this thing between us will not last.'

'You don't have to do anything.' Christine told him. 'Those are tears of happiness and you can enjoy them.'

'I'd surrender my heart if I knew where it was. Before this I was in some chamber under ground and now I'm soaring up in the clouds.' Christine nodded. 'It's not a sure thing, the clouds,' he said, wishing it were not true.

'No,' she replied quietly and taking him to the window they looked up to the sky, expecting to see their hearts up there, dancing in the clouds. She felt his hand in hers.

'Will we get back down again?' he asked and he cast his eyes down as though the earth were far below him.

The young girl kissed him long and sweetly to keep the charm alive and his confidence growing.

'I get startled,' Neil told her, taking a breath. 'First it was Cordelia's singing that caused the startlement and now it's you. I can't but wonder how the ground will ever stop from shaking if I do not have you by my side. The loss of you will make a drama out of standing still.'

'Well, you may yet have me closer than at your side,' Christine told him, 'and I have no plans to make a short season of it.'

Neil kissed her and Christine again sensed the strength of his neck and the rhythm of his chest. He would make real her tentative dreaming, that longing in her that had previously no more substance than dusty particles, and she'd know for certain that there's more to life than the bleak and dreary notion she'd recently had of it.

Awakened by Music

Clyde was in a dream, a dream that Cordelia's singing had stirred in him. He wandered in a daze talking quietly to himself and then drifted from the hall and up the stairs to his room.

'It's better to contemplate the meaning of these things alone,' he told himself, but no sooner had he opened the door than he heard a noise directly behind him. He turned suddenly and upon seeing Flora, he jumped, then Flora jumped.

In his after-years it was Clyde's *most vivid impression that her eyes had first given him the embarrassment that kept him dumb in her presence for a minute after she had come upon him thus strangely ensconced in the dark corridor. It was those eyes – the eyes of the woman born and bred by seas unchanging yet never the same; unfathomable, yet always inviting to the guess, the passionate surmise – that told him first here was a maiden made for love. A figure tremulous with a warm grace, a countenance perfect in its form, full of natural gravity, yet quick to each emotion, turning from the pallor of sudden alarm to the flush of shyness or vexation. The mountains had stood around to shelter her and she was like the harebell of the hills. Had she been the average of her sex he would have met her with a front of brass; instead there was confusion in his utterance and his mien. He bowed extremely low.*

'Madam; pardon! I – I – was awakened by music, and...'

Her silence, unaccompanied even by a smile at the ridiculous nature of the rencontre and the proud sobriety of her visage quickened him to a bolder sentiment than he had at first meditated.

'I was awakened by music, and it seems appropriate. With Madame's permission I shall return to earth.'

His foolish words perhaps did not quite reach her: the wind eddied noisily in the stair that seemed, in the light from his open door, to gulp the blackness. Perhaps she did not hear, perhaps she did not fully understand, for she hesitated more than a moment as if pondering, not a whit astonished or abashed, with her eyes upon his countenance. Clyde *wished to God that he had lived a cleaner life: somehow he felt that there were lines upon his face betraying him.* [30]

Flora's heart was in her eyes, even Clyde could see that, but he stepped back slowly as if making a move to enter his room.

'I was just...' he began and stopped, not knowing what he should say to explain himself.

The girl saw he was bound to go. He was as restless as if the snow was a swarm of seangans. She had not two drops of blood in her lips, but she tried to laugh as she took something from her pocket and half held it out to him. He did not understand at first, for if he was smart on the caman ball, 'twas slow in the ways of women he was.

'It's daft I am. I don't know what it is, but I had a dream that wasn't canny last night, and I'm afraid,' said the poor girl. 'I was going to give you ... '

Clyde *could not get the meaning of the laugh, strained as it was. He thought the maid's reason was wandering. She had, whatever it was – a square piece of cloth of a woman's sewing – into the man's hand before he knew what she would be after; and when his fingers closed on it* he felt a coin.[31]

He held it up and saw there an ancient piece of the king's gold. Flora's eyes sparkled and Clyde understood everything then. First he kissed the gold and then he kissed Flora. So gentle was the feeling they shared, they could have been floating.

Too Much to Lose

Annie stared straight ahead as though she were lost in a mist and had to strain her eyes to see what lay before her. Sebastian gazed at her profile. 'Is she very beautiful?' he asked himself and then he provided the anwer. 'She is more beautiful than any portrait of antiquity.' His need of her attention being great, he asked Annie what was occupying her thoughts so completely.

'I am not thinking at all,' was Annie's reply. 'Cordelia's singing made me completely happy and now... well, now you ask it, I am thinking. I am thinking about France.'

Sebastian gave a start. 'France,' he cried in jubilation, 'that is my country,' and taking up her hand he *started to tell her of rich and rolling fields, flat and juicy, waving to the wind; of country houses lost and drowned among flowers.* 'And all the roads lead one way,' said he, 'to a *great and sparkling town. Rain or shine, there is comfort, and there is the happy heart! The windows open on the laughing lanes, and the girls look out and lean after us, who prance by on our horses. There is the hollow hearty hoof-beat on the causey stones; in the halls the tables gleam with silver and gold; the round red apples roll over the platter among the slim-stemmed wine-beakers. It is the time of soft talk and the head full of gallant thoughts. Then there are the nights warm and soft, when the open doors let out the laughing and the gliding of silk-shooned feet, and the airs come in heavy with the scent of breckan and tree.'*[32]

'On my word,' said Annie, 'but it's like a girl's dream and the place is always as I have thought of it.'

Then, with no further impetus to promote it, something of Arcadian simplicity flew between them and they kissed; the knowledge of it filled them with surprise, just as an unknown jewel stolen might startle a thief. They felt such value in their lips that it drew out their spirits and the cascading loveliness was so great that it reminded Annie of the kind of festooning silver sparkles that shower down from the sky on firework night. They had never felt so confident and complete as they did then, but for Annie the ecstasy was short lived. Her delightful revery was interrupted by the realisation that in the morning she must get about her business as a singer in a band.

'I have responsibilities,' she said sorrowfully, 'and tomorrow I must tear myself away from this beautiful place and return to France.'

'France!' he cried, delighted. 'This is ravishing news ... '

'Yes?' she answered dubiously, reddening a little, and wondered why he should particularly think so.

'Ma foi! It is,' he insisted heartily. 'I had the most disturbing visions of your wandering elsewhere.'[33]

'And where might that place be?'

'Well anywhere that separated you from me, but

if France is where you're headed then we will return together. I could never find happiness if I were ever again far from the beating of your heart.'

'But I'm going to Toulouse,' Annie said, making the destination sound hopeless.

'Perfect,' he cried. *He felt exaltation simply at the prospect. To see her there! To have a host's right to bid her welcome to his land, this fair wild-flower.* [33] 'Then to Toulouse we shall go. I have too much to lose to lose you in Toulouse,' *and he caught her hand that trembled in his like a bird.* 'Annie! – *Oh God, the name is like a song – Je t'aime! Je t'aime!* Annie, *I love you.*' [33]

Annie laughed, astounded that she had discovered her Frenchman so far from the place of her yearning. Very tentative it was when she began her singing and it continued soft and quiet so that no-one would hear it but Sebastian, and it came to him while he was kissing the salty little tears that sparkled in her eyes.

A Salve for a Sore Heart

Cordelia's singing filled Aileen with an overwhelming desire to dance. Why dancing she did not know, but she wanted to hold a man to her bosom and dance with him about the hall 'til the whole world disappeared, 'til nothing existed but her and her partner and they were moving in harmony at one with the rhythms that now inhabited her bones.

It was Lindsay, Eilidh's artist, who happened to be standing next to Aileen, and when she turned to him and he held up his arms, welcoming her to hold him, it was as though he understood her every desire; more, it was as though his own desire to dance was entirely in accord with hers.

The happy couple glided softly around the room with their eyes closed and it wasn't until they had arrived on the terrace that they opened them again. They looked into each other's eyes and there was nothing for it but to honour their feelings with a kiss. It was a moment's kiss, fleeting, but it said everything. They held each other's gaze, no more than a few inches apart, and Aileen ran her hand across Lindsay's chest. She felt something there that hung from his neck by a ribbon and lifting it she saw a curious harp that was not altogether a harp.

'*What hast here?' asked* Aileen.

'*A salve for a sore heart,' he said. 'I can play on it some old tunes, and by the magic of it I'm back in my father's home and unafeared.'*

He drew his white fingers over the strings and made a thin twittering of music sweeter than comes from the clarsach-strings, but foreign and uncanny. To Aileen *it brought notions of far-off affairs, half sweet, half sad, like the edges of dreams and the moods that come on one in loneliness and strange places, and one tune he played was a tune she had heard* many times before.[34]

'That's a song my mother used to sing to us when we were children,' she said, 'but she never could sing the whole of it.'

'*Let me sing you a song,' said he, 'all for yourself.'*

'*You are a bard?' she said, with a pleased face.*

He said nothing, but touched on the curious harp, and sang to Aileen's *eyes, to the spark of them and the dance of them and the deep thought lurking in their corners, to her lips crimson like the rowan and curled with pride, to the set of breast and shoulder, and the voice melting on the tongue.*

It was all in the tune and the player's looks, for the words were fairy to Aileen, *but so plain the story, her face burned, and her eyes filled with a rare confusion.*

'It is the enchantment of fairydom,' said she. 'Am not I the oinseach to listen? I'll warrant you have sung the same to many a poor girl in all airts of the world?'[34]

Lindsay laughed and lifting his lips close to Aileen's

he told her that he would be content to sing to her for all time. *Then he kissed her with hot lips; his breath was in her hair; enchantment fell on her like a plaid, but she tore herself away.*[34]

'I am a grandmother, for goodness sake,' she told him reprovingly, 'and if you are going to kiss me like that you had better be doing it in private.'

'At your suggestion I could be anywhere.'

'Well home is the only place I know of.'

'I could just lift you in my arms and carry you all the way home,' he cried.

'Then I shall make a run for it and if you are still at your craving you can follow at my heels as fast as your legs will carry you.'

And with that, she opened a gate and was off up the track before Lindsay had even the thought to follow her. Seconds later the good man made his start and soon after that he held her in his arms.

In a Flame of Colour

At the start of the singing Alastair *felt the weariness of the past week's doings mount on him; he was a little dazed, his mind in a half delirium. And then of a sudden he was wide awake, with the beachdair of him uppermost!* [35]

'Now there's singing that could move the stars,' he declared and Kirsty at his side agreed with him.

'Are you a romantic man, Alastair?' she asked.

'Aye,' came his reply. 'There's not a bit of me in this landscape that doesna know the romance of it.'

'I have the landscape in me too,' she told him. 'I was, after all, conceived in an inn on the *God-forgotten, manforsworn, wild Rannoch. The inn stood on a desert edge; behind rose up the scowling mountains of Glen Coe, so high and steep that even the heather failed them, and their gullies sent down streams of stones instead of foam. Eastward, where the inn-front looked, the moor stretched flat and naked as a sound; all untracked and desert melancholy.* It is near Loch Ba. Perhaps you know it?'

'*I know every creek of that same loch,*' said he, '*and every wee bit ealan on it. It is alive with fish; it is the nursery of Tummel and Tay, – it is the mother of floods; there is for me no fonder place in great Breadalbane, and many a day a ghost of me is standing there upon its shore, remembering, remembering.'*³⁵

'Aye, I too have ghosts in this place. My mother waited long for my father to return to her there, but he never came. First it was his fishing that kept him away and then it was the war. She never forgave him, but if I ever asked after him she would sing me a sweet song about this man who was my father. Alastair was his name and suddenly, with you here, I have the notion that he might be you.'

'Tach!' said Alastair. *'That's a woman's reason, and there's no' much in it. Half the blunders people make come out of thinking life is like a story or a song.'*³⁵

It was Alastair's sudden fearfulness that prompted this response, for it's certain that he believed otherwise. In Kirsty's *manner were uneasiness and restraint. From him to her there was conveyed some influence bodiless and secret – hints and premonstrations in his flattest tones, the twitching of his eyebrows, even in the breathing of his nostrils. His air affected her peculiarly.*³⁵

'But you're the right age and I could swear there is something between us, certainly around the eyes.'

Alastair *rubbed his chin. 'My loss!' said he, 'that your mother is not to the fore; she maybe could have understood ye! Ye beat me!'*³⁵

'But think,' Kirsty pleaded, 'do you have no memory of a tryst to return to a woman in this place?'

*'All I have got is the twig the fish were on.'*³⁵

'You've more than that, for I'm tellin' ye I could be the fish,' Kirtsy cried and with this Alastair froze.

'Tha airgiod ann! – There's money in it!' said he, with

125

some crazy[35] notion of possible mercenary intentions.

'*Oh,' she cried, and wrung her hands, 'that's just what tortures me! I want no father who's under an obligation, or might think he was!'*

She flung from the room in a rage of indignation[35] and Alastair, with deep regret flung himself after her.

'*Stop, stop!' he cried, ashamed; 'you go too fast for me. For all that there is between us – just a word!'*

Kirsty, having no ambition to get beyond his reach, allowed him to come by, but she wanted to punch him.

'*There's not much need for words at the age of you; it's in the eyes* and I have seen enough. I hate you.'

'My lass,' he cried, 'I love you,' and stretching towards her *the upper buttons of his waistcoat burst; he was inflamed and swollen with injured pride. She picked up one that fell to the floor and polished it along her sleeve; she stood abashed like a little child.*

'*You put me to shame, father!' she cried.*

'*Yes,' he cried, 'and you put me to my shame.'*[35]

'Thank heavens there's still time,' she said.

The Soaring Lark

It was something like a sob he heard first, a faint sound, but it was enough to wake him from his enchantment. James turned to Esther and seeing the tears in her eyes his heart went out to her and he told himself that here were the wellings of that strange chagrin that comes on all the sensitive who know that beauty is brief. He wanted nothing but to hold her to him.

'Your tears come quickly on this happy occasion,' he said, not knowing what else he might say. 'Please say they are not mixed with sorrow.'

'Sorrow? No,' she replied. 'My tears could know nothing of sorrow after such singing, but...' and she stopped briefly, 'but it's just possible that I should admit to feeling, well... that the singing could have made me just a little forlorn.'

'Forlorn,' said James *passionate. 'Whoever can be moved by days and scenes like these can never be for long forlorn;' and then of a sudden there came to him, as he saw the curve of her neck, the throb of her bosom, the conviction that the world without her would indeed be desolate. Now he knew the gossamer web that lay between him and the complete surrender of the soaring lark, the*

unalterable contentment of stars forever inseparable. ³⁶

'Is it possible,' he asked, 'that we could simply decide to be together for as long as the stars continue to shine?' And his words surprised him.

'That I can't guess,' Esther replied quietly and, looking up to the ceiling as though the stars were hidden there, she felt his hand in hers and she dropped her gaze to him. No words came to her, so James broke the silence.

'I love you and I want to...' he began, but Esther placed her fingers on his lips.

'Please not yet... do not say it yet,' and looking into his eyes she saw such happiness of anticipation there that she cast her own eyes down. 'These things just don't happen to me,' she said. She was half pleading with him to break the charm that lay between them and half desiring that they could keep it alive forever.

'These things don't happen to me either,' he declared, passionate, 'but now they have, you might exchange your tears for laughter and pay the feelings some tribute.'

'But I cannot imagine how it would occur and now... oh now I am going to cry again and just because I really am so happy and what else can I do?'

Esther turned away and James *looked at the swell of her throat and the surge of her breasts where the primrose lay, and felt again that yearning aimless and serene. A thousand times had come to him in happy hours a brief conviction that between him and bliss's very climax something less tangible than a web of gossamer lay; but how to break through these bounds, that were on trial more durable than ramparts of stone! Now the sense of it was in every artery; his heart, he felt, was tangled in her hair, though he never had the thought in words but in a shiver of his being. He saw that she was what he once had thought the world was – in its morning, before the curst sophistications. The boat song floated over the sea, the linnet piped on land, the waters were blue to very ecstasy – the very heaven itself.*

She had been looking before her into the west, out to the far horizon, as if her thoughts were there, content in all her being, her eyes half closed on a dazzle of waves, her lips scarcely parted. [36]

James turned her to him and held her with his eyes, so adamant that she knew why she should be happy.

'That's it then,' she said. 'There is nothing to be done, we are in love.' Together they swayed, guided by the same spirit, as though an oirram of the ancient unperplexed old days was directing their movement and the world about them all but disappeared in a haze of light.

Running on Fairy Isles

Eilidh was close enough to Emile to touch his arm and when she did he gave a start. The couple looked intently at each other and then they laughed.

'I am sorry to have been the cause of your disturbance,' she said at last calmly, *in a voice with the music of lulled little waves running on fairy isles in summer weather, almost without trace that English was not her natural tongue, and that faint innuendo of the mountain melody but adding to the charm of her accent.*

'There is positively not the necessity,' protested Emile.

'But you showed such startlement that I thought you were...'

'The explanation is due from me, Madame: I protest,' said he, and she pouted. It gave her a look so bewitching, so much the aspect of a tempest bound in a cobweb that he was compelled to smile, and for the life of her she could not but respond with a similar display. It seemed, when he saw her smile through her clouds that he had wandered blindly through the world till now. France, far-off in sunshine, brimming with laughter and song, its thousand interests, its innumerable happy associations,

were of little account to the fact that now he was under the same roof with a woman who charmed magic flutes and who endowed the dusks with mystery and surprise.[37]

It was no matter to Emile now if the crumbling walls of this castle hummed with the incessant wind and the vibration of the tempestuous sea, for now, this very second, he was in paradise and if need be he would stay here with her forever.

He tried again to voice the explanation he had promised earlier and was perplexed that he could not. For reasons that were quite similar, Eilidh also had the emotional hesitancy in her manner; she could not remember the last time her voice had been so difficult to find.

She bit her nether lip – the orchards of Cramercy, Emile *told himself, never bred a cherry a thousandth part so rich and so inviting even to look at in candle-light; a shy dubiety hovered round her eyes. He waited her pleasure to speak.*

'Perhaps,' said she softly, relinquishing her brave demeanour – 'perhaps one day I could visit you in France.'

'Madam,' said Emile, '*I am – what do you call it? – a somnambulist. In that condition it has sometimes been my so good fortune to wander into the most odd and ravishing situation. But as it happens, helas! I can never recall a single incident of them when I waken in the morning.*[37] What I fear now is that I am truly fast asleep and you and all this are only a dream.'

Eilidh laughed. 'It would give me the greatest pleasure to join you in your nocturnal wanderings,' she told him.

'I have all the necessary qualities – romance, enterprise and an appetite for adventure.'

'But would you stay? I mean if you came to France, would you stay with me there? If it were just a holiday I doubt that I could bear to depart from you.'

'Mai oui, but of course,' Eilidh replied, and she hugged him and kissed him and laughed.

'But what of your bookshop, what will happen to that without you there to run it?'

Eilidh assumed the expression of thinking deep to give Emile the impression that she had not until this moment considered the matter – a contrivance that was far from the truth. Emile gazed at her, waiting anxiously for her words and Eilidh held out on her reply until she felt that the smile on her face must now give her game away.

'Och, it's time Flora had the use of it,' she said, with as much nonchalance as she could muster, 'but not tonight, my dear, tonight my little house will be ours.'

Where Comes no Grief or Ageing

Mairi and Andrew stood together, hand-in-hand gazing at their star-struck guests.

'So tell me,' he asked his new wife, 'do you now feel that your wedding was a success?'

'In everything,' she told him and then, stopping to show that she was still thinking, she added, 'but one thing.'

Andrew laughed and kissed her. 'And what,' he asked 'might this one thing be?

'Our honeymoon,' she told him. 'We did not plan a honeymoon for ourselves.'

'But surely,' said he, surprised, 'there are no finer places for love then here?'

Of course there were the little dells close on the wider bay where it was possible to sit upon the sand and love as the bird loves, unnoticed. But only Mairi *knew that and she did not tell, for to be seen on any day but a festival coming from these sandy hollows was the unfailing sign that weddings were at hand. But there was the little Ron, the fairy boat. No hesitation need be about the pair of them sailing out to Tir-nan-oig, for no-one knew but themselves that Tir-nan-oig was there, and often* Andrew, *in that cheerful spring, would take the tiller, and she snug up beside him, glad in his arm, desirable exceedingly, her voice in his bosom. The Ron – the Seal, unfitting name for this good boat, this galley of joy! It should have been the Eala Bhan – the wild white swan, proud strong bird of the islands, and beautiful and free, – the Ron swam in these days round the coast and into lonely creeks, where only, from the cliffs, the fulmer's cry was to be heard, its wedding song. Long and far would they glide silent through the waters into shallows where brown burns from the bog-lands stained the froth of tides incoming, and birds twittered among the shelisters and sedges, and little fish plowted in the pools, and the spout-fish thrust from the sand, parched with the sun, but seemingly finding the heat delightful. Silent, the two of them, like as it were a swound they sailed in and she could hear his heart beating at her ear.* [38]

'*What do you say, my dear, to Tir-nan-oig?*' Andrew asked and Mairi, smiling, took his hand and pulled him from the hall.

They fled the sound of the revellers and together launched the Ron. She sat in his arm and heard again his heart beat at her ear and felt his breath in her hair and over him there came the birchen odour. A half-moon swung like a halberd-head among the stars; the Sound was filled with gold. Along the shores the little waves went lapping softly; burns tinkled down the sands. For long they sailed in silence, indulgent of their illusion that this indeed was Tir-nan-oig, where comes no grief or ageing. They rounded the cove and heard the whooper swan in his sleep; the night was generous of its memories that came to them often again when they saw their children sail in the bay.

'And did you imagine that for lack of planning no honeymoon would be yours?' Andrew asked and Mairi ceased her gazing at the stars then.

She nestled in his arms. 'I did not, dear,' said she. 'Were we not together once in Tir-nan-oig? Who comes back from Tir-nan-oig?

The Ron – oh happy galley! Surely no other boat in all the world bore freight more precious than these two hearts – swam through the liquid gold; jewels from the deep came beaded on her sides and broke profuse and glowing at her bow. William and Annabel were down by the foreshore and they waved to the happy couple. *'Mairi is satisfied,' said they, sharing her happiness. They heard her sing. Her voice came over the water from Orosay's lee, a sound enchanting – Bride's voice that hushes the children and wrings the hearts of men.* [38]

References to the Novels of Neil Munro

Unless otherwise stated all novels are published by William Blackwood & Sons. For the most part I have quoted from a series referred to as the Inverary Edition, but when I have quoted from earlier additions I give the numbered edition.

THE GATHERING

1. *Gilian The Dreamer*, 1936, page 66
2. *Fancy Farm*, 1949, pages 5 and 6
3. *Doom Castle*, 1948, page 14
4. *Gilian The Dreamer*, 1936, page 232
5. *The New Road*, 1950, pages 62 and 63
6. *Gilian The Dreamer*, 1936, pages 252 and 253
7. *The Lost Pibroch*, 1898, Second Edition, page 1
8. *A Return To Nature*, from *Jaunty Jock*, 1948, page 159
9. *The Brooch*, from *Jaunty Jock*, 1948, page 178
10. *Para Handy*, published by Berlin Limited, 2002, page 42
11. *Fancy Farm*, 1949, page 188
12. *Gilian The Dreamer*, 1936, pages 45 and 46
13. *John Splendid*, 1899, Sixth Edition, page 242
14. *The Lost Pibroch*, 1898, Second Edition, page 20
15, 16, 17   *Children Of Tempest*, First Edition, 1903, pages 14, 28 and 5
18. *The Lost Pibroch*, 1898, Second Edition, page 10
19. *The Lost Pibroch*, 1898, Second Edition, page 11 and 12
20. *The Lost Pibroch*, 1898, Second Edition, page 13, 14 and 18
21, 22, 23   *The Shoes Of Fortune*, 1935, pages 61, 57 and 70
24, 25   *John Splendid*, 1899, Sixth Edition, pages 275 and 278
26. *The Sea-Fairy Of French Foreland*, from *The Lost Pibroch*, 1898, Second Edition, page 161
27. *The Daft Days*, 1948, page 96

THE WEDDING

28 *Gilian The Dreamer*, 1936, page 111
29 *Burns And Clarinda*, from *Ayrshire Idylls*, 1948, page 282
30 *Doom Castle*, 1948, page 117
31 *Shudderman Soldier*, from *The Lost Pibroch*, 1898, Second Edition, page 179
32 *The Sea-Fairy Of French Foreland*, from *The Lost Pibroch*, 1898, Second Edition, pages 164 and 165
33 *Doom Castle*, 1948, pages 281, 283 and 288
34 *The Sea-Fairy Of French Foreland*, from *The Lost Pibroch*, 1898, Second Edition, pages 167 and 168
35 *The New Road*, 1950, pages 308, 88, 331, 311, 329, 325, 309, 329 and 328
36 *Children Of Tempest*, First Edition, 1903, pages 126 and 125
37 *Doom Castle*, 1948, pages 118, 119 and 120
38 *Children Of Tempest*, First Edition, 1903, pages 145 and 146, 295 and 296